D0454827

FAMILY MATTERS

FAMILY MATTERS

A Novel

IRA BERKOWITZ

KATE'S MYSTERY BOOKS
JUSTIN, CHARLES & CO., PUBLISHERS
BOSTON

FIRST EDITION

ISBN10: 1-932112-44-8
ISBN13: 978-1-932112-44-3

Library of Congress Cataloging-in-Publication is available.

Published in the United States by Kate's Mystery Books,
an imprint of Justin, Charles & Co., Publishers,
Boston, Massachusetts
www.justincharlesbooks.com

2 4 6 8 10 9 7 5 3 1

PRINTED IN THE UNITED STATES OF AMERICA

FOR PHYLLIS
ALWAYS AND FOREVER

I wish to thank the following people without whose help this book would never have seen the light of day.

With unending patience, unsparing generosity, and sorely needed encouragement, Roberta Silman, a very gifted writer and teacher, steered me past the potholes, read every revision, and taught me how to write. I am forever grateful for her friendship.

My thanks also to my agent, Gina Panettieri, who took a chance on a first-time writer and proivided encouragement, insight, and valuable advice along the way.

Thanks also to Stephanie Abrutyn who helped me navigate the legal minefields.

This is a book about family, and I want to acknowledge mine. Daniel, Robin, David, Allison, and Michael have brought me more joy than any person has a right to expect.

Finally, this book is for my parents. They would have been proud.

FAMILY MATTERS

CHAPTER ONE

April 2004 — New York City

He sensed this day would finally come, and now that it had, he greeted it with great anticipation. This would be a special day, the start of another great adventure.

After a breakfast of creamy scrambled eggs, lightly buttered toast, and coffee, he straightened the apartment, made his bed, showered, dressed, and went out. It was a glorious day, a day to revel in beginnings. High, scudding clouds moved across the face of the sun so swiftly that the flat winter light appeared to vibrate.

He had planned every detail carefully. His first stop was Coppola's barbershop on Tenth, where ten dollars bought a first-class haircut and the closest shave any man would ever want. Angelo Coppola waved him into the chair next to the window, giving him an unobstructed view of the street.

"The usual?" Angelo asked. It was the same question he had asked every week for over fifty years, and the response was always the same.

"Sure, a trim and a shave."

Angelo draped a sheet over his friend's torso, pulled

1

a pair of scissors from the pocket of his smock, and went to work shaping the thick shock of gray hair.

"So how're things going, Ange?"

"Terrific! I'm supporting a shylock who looks like the third guy from the left in the evolutionary chart, I take two steps and I need a nap, and business sucks. Other than that, I'm in the pink. But this you gotta hear. I bet this horse running at Yonkers. Far and away the class of the field. Went big on him. Can't miss, right?" Angelo said.

He waited for the punch line.

"The fucker *bled!* Could you believe it? With all the other shit you got to worry about, like track condition and times and whether the jock is down on another nag in the race, I got a horse that bled, for Chrissakes. At the half-mile post the fucker collapsed and died. Never seen anything like it in my life. It got me to thinking. Screw win, place, and show. They ought to have a window where you can bet whether the horse fucking *lives.*"

He smiled. "Do you think the Giants win ten games this year, Ange?"

"I'm through with them," he said, tucking the scissors back in his pocket. "I coulda sent all three of my kids to college on the money I lost on those lay down artists." He stepped back to check his work. "You're good," he pronounced, without asking for confirmation. He adjusted the chair, and his old friend closed his eyes and lay back.

Angelo reached into a silvery globe, plucked out a steaming towel, and wrapped it around his friend's face, leaving only his nose exposed.

2

"Too hot?" Angelo asked.

His friend muttered something that sounded like "no." When the towel hit his face, the muscles went slack, and the only sound he heard was a muffled strop as Angelo honed the straight razor.

Angelo removed the towel and applied the lather, working it into the bristles. With deft strokes he scraped until the skin was as smooth as fine silk. Finally, he splashed some Pinaud on his hands and patted it on his friend's face.

He came out of the chair, reached into his pocket and brought out a fifty, palmed it, and tucked it into Angelo's pocket. "You take care now, Ange," he said. He was feeling on top of the world.

His next stop was Chase Bank. He walked down a flight of stairs to the vault. A pretty, young woman with auburn hair and laughing eyes sat at the desk. He signed the register and handed her the key to his safe-deposit box. He retrieved the box, opened it in her presence, and removed its only contents, a gray manila envelope. He handed her the empty box. "God, you're pretty," he said. "I wish I were fifty years younger . . ."

A blush crept up from her throat and she smiled. "I wish you were, too."

He patted her cheek. "Ah, more's the pity."

He left Chase and walked east to Fifth Avenue. It was choked with people. At Fifty-seventh Street he turned west until he reached Cressgil & Smith. He entered the store and asked for a bottle of Aberlour single-malt scotch.

"You've got good taste," the sandy-haired young

clerk said. He wore chinos, and the sleeves of his yellow shirt were rolled up over his elbows.

The price was outrageous, but it was a rare indulgence. "Nothing but the best for a special day," he said.

The clerk retrieved the bottle and placed it on the counter. "Are you familiar with its history?"

He was, but the clerk was so earnest, he let him tell it.

"Well, the water comes from a natural spring in Ben Rinnes, Scotland. Legend has it that hundreds of years ago a saint, Drostan I think, baptized the people of the town with it."

"Do you believe it?" he said.

The clerk shrugged. "Why not?"

"A good answer," he said. "Then let's proclaim it a holy drink. Fit for absolution and the washing away of sin."

"I never thought of it that way," the clerk said, ringing up the transaction and placing the bottle into a small plastic shopping bag imprinted with the store's logo.

When he returned home, he set the Abelour and the envelope on a side table and walked into the kitchen. He took a tumbler from a cabinet and rinsed it with hot water. With a dishtowel he rubbed it until it gleamed, then set it on the table next to the Abelour. The sun streamed in through the window, backlighting the bottle and turning the scotch to glowing amber. Just looking at it made his mouth dry from want.

He walked into the bedroom and undressed, neatly hanging his clothes in the closet. Reaching into the back, he removed his uniform and laid it on the bed. Then he dressed. It was tight, but he managed. He stepped into a pair of highly polished shoes and walked to the mirror for an inspection. His gold detective's shield gleamed.

Satisfied, he went back to the living room and settled into his easy chair. He unsealed the bottle of Aberlour, poured the liquid into the tumbler, and inhaled the aroma of fruit and spice mixed with honey. He lifted it to his lips and sipped. It was creamy and smooth, just as he remembered. Small sips, he reminded himself. To do anything else would be sacrilege.

He put the tumbler down and glanced at the two framed photographs sitting on top of the TV. There was one of him and his wife on their wedding day, and the other with the boys on a party boat out of Sheepshead Bay. They had gone for blues. It was a good day. A fishing trip didn't make a father, his wife had scolded. And a marriage license didn't make a husband, he thought. Things didn't turn out the way he had expected. Life sometimes got in the way. He sighed, but this wasn't the time for regrets.

He took another small sip of Aberlour and opened the manila envelope and removed its contents: a black leather-bound notebook and a thick bundle of letters. He read the letters first, in chronological order. In half an hour he was finished. As little as he had to drink, he felt the scotch working into his bloodstream. The skin on his face grew tighter, his tongue thicker. He felt good. At peace. Setting the letters in his lap, he picked up the notebook. He read it all the way through, and then read it again. He reached over to the end table and retrieved the two objects he had set out the night before, a Xerox copy of a photo and his service revolver.

It was time.

After filling the tumbler to the top, he drained it. It tasted like morning sun. Then he lifted the revolver, stuck the muzzle in his mouth, and pulled the trigger.

CHAPTER TWO

February 2004 — New York City

The one true thing Steeg knew was this: There was nothing usual about Hell's Kitchen.

He had been asleep dreaming candy apple dreams when a siren bit through the night like an ax blade. He didn't know why, but in that moment he sensed that the order of things had changed. The way his life was going, it wasn't a surprise.

Steeg dragged himself out of bed and went to the window. In the street below, cops swarmed into his apartment house like a troop of army ants. He threw on the clothes he had left in a pile a few hours before and walked down the stairs to the third-floor landing. Professional curiosity, he rationalized. Bullshit, he retorted.

All the activity was focused on Graham Moore's apartment, directly beneath his. Steeg strolled in as if he belonged and looked around. The scene was a basic NYPD cluster fuck. There were cops thrilled to be out of the cold for a few minutes and trying to look busy, crime scene investigators setting up their equipment, and a couple of sergeants barking orders at anyone further down the pay scale.

The apartment was a pit. If Moore were going for a welfare hotel "look," he had clearly succeeded. The one-bedroom railroad flat appeared to have been decorated by Goodwill, a celebration of the mismatched and drab: a nubby gray sofa, a few sorry-looking, cane-backed chairs, an old RCA on a tubular chrome stand, and a couple of Holiday Inn rustic scenes hanging on walls painted the color of lichen.

Moore was nowhere in sight.

As Steeg walked toward the bedroom, he drew a handkerchief from his pocket and held it to his nose. After fifteen years investigating homicides, he still hadn't gotten used to the smell of death. But he could tell when it had happened with a fair degree of accuracy. Putrefaction worked on its own timetable.

Two days, he concluded.

Give or take.

"Can I help you?" The voice was reedy and uncertain.

The nametag attached to the voice read EDMONDS. He was young, smooth-cheeked, and barely out of the Academy. From his post at the door, Edmonds's job was to keep civilians out. He had screwed up, but it was an honest mistake. Everything about Steeg said "cop." He was tall and rangy, with aquamarine eyes that could go from amused to deadly in a heartbeat. The problem was that Steeg wasn't a cop, at least not officially. He was two months into a six-month suspension, and his gold shield sat in a drawer at One Police Plaza.

"Can I help you?" Edmonds repeated.

Steeg was ready to call it a night. He had learned everything he needed to know. Someone was dead. Curiosity satisfied. Time to go. It wasn't his business anymore. But what lay behind the bedroom door tugged at him.

Stay or go? The inviting prospect of a warm bed, or a chance to peek through the curtains of Door Number One?

"Screw it!" he muttered. He turned to Edmonds. "Who found the vic?" His tone was direct and official without being officious. Very cop-like.

It was enough to convince Edmonds.

"The super," he said, jerking his chin at a short, wiry Hispanic man leaning uncomfortably against the windowsill. Fading tattoos of the Virgin and bleeding saints covered his thin arms. "One of the neighbors complained about the smell."

Steeg glanced over at Luis Santos, who clearly wished he were somewhere else.

"Did you get a statement?"

"Uh — Sergeant Petrov —"

Steeg cut Edmonds off. "What about I.D.?"

"Like I was saying, Sergeant Petrovitch probably . . ."

Steeg noticed that Wayne Petrovitch, the proximate reason for his suspension, was poking around in the refrigerator searching for a late-night snack. It figured.

"I'll get it later," Steeg said.

He turned his back on Edmonds and walked into the bedroom.

No one paid any attention.

The early poverty motif was repeated there. A metal

snack table doubled as a nightstand. A dark wood chifforobe had drawers that didn't quite fit on one side, while
Armani and Zegna suits hung from wire hangers on the
other. Walls painted the same pukey color as the living
room. And on the bed, a young, naked woman with small
breasts and creamy white skin lay faceup on tangled
sheets. Mid to late twenties, Steeg thought. Blond hair
cut fashionably short. Softly pretty. Fingernails neatly
trimmed and buffed. Makeup meticulously applied. A
woman careful about her appearance. A woman out of
place in Hell's Kitchen.

Steeg felt the familiar gut-tightening sensation that
invariably came with his first look at any homicide victim. They were all blank pages. And this one was no different. No visible signs of bruising. Skin toneless and
waxy gray. Lips pulled tight against her teeth in a frozen
rictus of vacant surprise, as if she had starred in a moral-
ity play with a trick ending. Or, did her expression cap-
ture that moment of certainty, the fatal epiphany when
the reassuring words of her killer revealed the lie?

Steeg had a feeling—more a premonition—that the expression frozen on her face was the first letter in the alphabet of her story. In the course of time, more letters
would be added, ultimately filling her page with the inevitable evasions, lies, and half-truths that constituted
her life. But for Steeg, the truth always hid in the white
space between the letters.

Still, it wasn't his business anymore.

"Doing your 'ting again, Jackson? Channelin' the
corpse?" The question was delivered in a smoky Louisiana patois.

Luce Guidry was the only one who called Steeg by his given name, the only one to get close enough to get through the wall he had spent a lifetime constructing.

Tall, slim, and delicately pretty, with skin the color of café au lait and hair done up in tight cornrows, Luce's tastes ran to clunky junk jewelry and soft pastels. "What brings you here, Luce?"

"You, mon. Pullin' the late shift. When I heard the call come through for your address, I called. No answer. Left a message. You didn't call back. I got worried. So I figured I'd stop by for a look-see. At three in the mornin', God's children should be sleepin' not traipsin' through a crime scene. You takin' care of yourself, Jackson?" Her question had a guarded tone.

Luce Guidry had put up with more of Steeg's baggage than he had a right to expect. His troubles with alcohol, the breakup with Ginny — through it all, Luce was there. No questions asked. And, she was the only cop he knew who didn't treat him like a contagion after his suspension. Cops are programmed with powerful tribal notions. In the calculus of the police force, a suspension means you're off the team, a pariah, a mirror in which the tribe sees its own reflection.

There was a time when Steeg imagined something that was a lot more than a work relationship with Luce. But their taste in gender ran in opposite directions, so they settled for the next best thing. Friendship.

Avoiding Luce's gaze, he looked down at the body. "Been off the sauce for a month, and it's safe to say that I'm doing a little better than her."

"Glad to hear it. Who is she?"

"Beats me, but this you've got to see." He took Luce's arm and walked her over to the chifforobe. "Why would somebody who looks like him and lives like this wear thousand-dollar suits?"

"You know him?"

"Not really. The guy is in his fifties, kind of paunchy, and dresses like he's thirty." He glanced at the body on the bed. "And what's he doing with someone who looks like her? It doesn't figure."

"All very good questions, but you better get your ass out of here before Braddock shows up."

Captain Gerard Braddock, Steeg's boss, had slapped him with the suspension. They didn't get along.

"What's he gonna do if he finds me, give me a stern talking-to?"

"Come on, Jackson, you don't need any more of the man's shit — you got enough of your own to deal with."

Steeg shrugged and changed the subject. "How's Cherise?"

"Out of my life," she said with a tight smile. "This time, I mean it." She grabbed Steeg's arm and propelled him toward the door. "And I don't want the same thing to happen to you."

"Petrovich deserved to get his ass kicked."

"I know, Jackson." Luce sighed. "He's a homopho-bic, misogynistic asshole, but there's fuck all you can do about it. And Braddock is his rabbi. There's no why or where — there just is. Since you've been gone, I've moved up to the number-one spot on his shit list. Just keep your head down, do your time, and it'll be like nothin' ever happened when you come back."

Steeg wasn't sure about the "coming back" part, but in the interim he didn't want to screw up Luce's life, too.

"What the fuck is everybody doing here?" The voice boomed through the apartment. "All uniforms out! I want *one* guy at the door to secure the scene. Everybody else back on the street. We got bodies all over the city."

"Oh, shit!" Luce said.

Everything about Gerard Braddock was oversized, from his florid red face to the size-twelve, thick-soled brogans he kicked ass with. Prematurely gray, Braddock was in his late thirties, several years younger than Steeg, and pegged as a comer by people in the Department who spent their time thinking about things like that.

Steeg didn't share their opinion. As far as he was concerned, everything about Braddock said "off the rack." He was an ordinary guy with an ordinary mind who derived extra-ordinary pleasure by causing misery to anyone beneath his pay grade.

Surrounded by a clutch of lieutenants and sergeants attaching themselves to him like remora eels, Braddock spotted Steeg coming out of the bedroom. "Look what the cat dragged in," he sneered. "What the fuck're *you* doing here?"

Steeg returned the sneer. "I live here."

"*Here*, as in this armpit?"

"No, 'here,' as in this building."

Braddock couldn't let it go. "You actually live in this shit box?"

Steeg had to agree that Braddock's assessment wasn't too far off. "Home is where the heart is."

"So, you're like one of them fire dogs who hears the

bell and just has to come running. Problem is, you don't belong here. I suspended your ass, and the way I see it, you're interfering with a criminal investigation. Contaminating a crime scene. In fact, I could haul your ass in, but what's the point?"

"'Pointless,' is something you've always been good at, Gerry."

Flushing, Braddock took a few steps toward him. "What's that supposed to mean?"

The apartment went still.

Steeg didn't give an inch.

"It's funny, your lips are flapping, but like always, nothing comes out," Steeg said. "Things never change."

He could see the fury building in Braddock's face, and was convinced he would take a swing at him. But to Steeg's surprise, the tension went out of Braddock's body and his mouth creased into a smile.

"I'm not going to take the bait, asshole. Not this time. Don't let the door hit you in the ass on the way out." He laughed, winking broadly to the crowd.

At the front door, Steeg stopped and turned back to Braddock. Petrovich stood next to him, joining in the fun.

"Just keep on walkin', Jackson," Luce whispered. "Don't do this."

It was good advice, but Steeg generally heeded his own counsel. He pointed at Petrovich. "He kicks the shit out of a prisoner, *my* prisoner, and I get suspended. How does that work? I know you didn't make it on brains, so the way I figure, he's got his nose up your ass, and you've got your nose up the Chief of Detective's ass, and so on up the line. Looks like we got a regular blue daisy chain working here. Is that about right, *Gerry?*"

Steeg didn't wait for an answer. Feeling a lot better than he had in a long time, he turned and walked out.

Returning to his apartment, he flopped onto the bed and pulled a pillow over his head. From force of habit, his hand reached for the reassuring curve of Ginny's body, hoping to find comfort or even safety there. A futile gesture. It wasn't in the cards. Not anymore.

With a disgusted shake of his head he rose and walked over to the window. Red flashes pulsing in time to the throbbing in his temples drifted up from Forty-eighth Street. "Fuck it!" he said. A generic, all-purpose comment directed at the NYPD, the horror story that brought them to his building, the landlord for cutting the heat off at 10:00 the night before, and the all-around sorry state of his life.

Dwarfed between mega piers and new high-rises, Steeg's window offered only an insular view of the city. No dark line of the Hudson. No twinkling lights of Broadway. Only up or down. But he refused to look down, knowing what was playing out in the street below. Squad cars, ambulances, flashing lights. Another Hell's Kitchen Passion Play.

In the distance, Steeg heard the sound of sirens dopplering through the streets on the way to their own Passion Plays. He drew the blinds closed.

It wasn't his business anymore.

CHAPTER THREE

Steeg's building, the Excelsior, was little different from neighboring tenements and former rooming houses sporting equally ambitious names that made up Hell's Kitchen. Squeezed between the expanding Theater District to the east, pricey Central Park West to the north, a tide of urban renewal sweeping up from Chelsea, and the Hudson River at its back, the neighborhood was a pressure cooker.

In earlier times, Hell's Kitchen was a sulfurous mix of breweries, factories, warehouses, and slaughterhouses built right up to the docks. Toss in a heavy dose of gangs preying on the Irish and German immigrants and you had combustion. Violence was so common that it inspired George Gershwin to compose "Slaughter on Tenth Avenue." He certainly had the neighborhood pegged.

In recent years the city fathers attempted to put a dress on a pig by renaming the area Clinton. They didn't get it and never would. While Hell's Kitchen was in the city, it never was *of* the city.

The cold was numbing and brittle, a perfect morning for herding reindeer on the Chukchi Peninsula, but another lousy day in New York City. Driven by a Canadian low-pressure system, an angry tide of low, dark clouds rolled in over the Hudson, a hopeless prelude to a day that promised to suck joy from the soul.

Steeg had never been much for sleep, but the events of the night before took it completely off the table. The victim's expression continued to haunt him. It was as if she'd suspected all along that her life would end that way but was still surprised that it had. Reading didn't help, and television was a joke. There were just so many infomercials a human being could watch without experiencing brain melt, although he did have his eye on a set of knives so sharp they could fell a forest. Music, usually a pretty good standby, didn't work, either. A drink, though inordinately appealing, wasn't in the cards. Just seven steps into the alcoholic's twelve-step dance, a drop back would have made him regret all the fun he had missed while struggling through the first six. So, at 7:00 a.m., Steeg was out in the street.

Rahim "Dman" Sutter, a seventeen-year-old thug wearing baggy pants riding low at the crotch and an XXX sweatshirt with the hood pulled down over his Rasta do stood across the street. His first customers of the day had yet to straggle up. Before Steeg's suspension, Dman had made himself scarce, preferring to ply his chosen profession in other areas of the Kitchen. But word had spread that Steeg had gone down, and Dman was eyeing him with newfound confidence. It was time for a come-to-Jesus talk with Dman, Steeg decided. Time to let him know that down didn't mean out.

Up the block, Herkie, a middle-aged white man dreaming crack dreams, dozed under a sheet of fecal-colored industrial padding while Miguel and Santo, two other local worthies, made their morning rounds picking through garbage for empties.

In the few lucid moments when his neurons weren't firing like Roman candles, Herkie was an interesting guy. He loved poetry, especially the War Poets, and had the uncanny knack of remembering every poem he had ever read. When low on cash, which was all the time, he would find a spot in Times Square and set up a sign challenging anyone to name a poem he couldn't recite. Apparently, Herkie had taught the subject for a time at Medgar Evers College. At a buck a shot, it would have been a thriving business if the receipts didn't find their way up his nose or in his arm.

And sitting on the stoop was tiny DeeDee Santos, resembling a coppery-skinned Pillsbury Dough Girl in her puffy white down parka. She was waiting for Steeg. At the sight of her, Steeg knew that all was well with the world.

Twelve-year-old DeeDee, the only child of Luis and Milagro Santos, was Steeg's new best friend. Milagro, tired of playing Luis's heavy bag during his alcohol-driven sparring sessions, had gone into the wind several years before, leaving DeeDee as a fill-in. Not a situation conducive to a happy childhood. Life in the Kitchen was hard enough without the added pressure of a family gone into the dumper.

Soon after Milagro had left, DeeDee had drifted into the streets, cutting school, getting into trouble, and having a high old time. Steeg's suspension left him with a lot of downtime, and he noticed the very pretty little girl with the very sad smile. It was hard not to. Wherever Steeg was, DeeDee was sure to be — seeming to appear out of nowhere, throwing him sidelong glances but keeping her distance, as if waiting for him to make the first move. At first he thought she was flirting, giving her prepubescent skills a test-drive. Eventually he realized that wasn't it, and a more potent realization began to stir, inchoate at first, but gradually taking on dimension. He recognized in DeeDee something he had failed to see in himself.

Loneliness.

He and DeeDee were adrift and looking for the same thing: safe mooring in a peaceful harbor. It took several months, but they connected. Steeg's motives were not entirely altruistic. Maybe, he reasoned, if DeeDee turned out all right, just maybe there was a chance for him, too.

Hunching his shoulders against the wind, Steeg sat down beside her. She smelled like summer. It was something intrinsically bound up in the biology of children. From the moment they're born, they exude the heady perfume of grass and flowers, but the day they lose their innocence, it's gone. Steeg wondered when that day would come for DeeDee.

"You look like crap, Steeg," she said. "Bad night?"

"Did you have breakfast yet?"

"Some left-over arroz con pollo."

"The breakfast of champions."

"Papi said he saw you last night. You know, in the apartment."

"Saw him, too."

"What happened?"

He glanced at his watch. "Isn't it time for school?"

She smiled at him playfully. "Maybe."

"What's that supposed to mean?"

"I'm burned out, Steeg. Seventh grade is a bitch. Why do I have to know all that history and math and shit? I ain't ever going to use it."

A 747 swung wide over the Hudson and doubled back for a landing at Newark, leaving icy vapor trails in its wake.

"Watch your mouth. You're too young to be burned out."

"I need a vacation."

"Me too."

"You're on one. You ain't a cop no more. 'Member?"

"Fair point." Steeg looked up; Dman was eyeballing them.

"Your bus is here, and you're going to be on it. Drop the attitude and grab your books."

"Aw." She groaned, rising to her feet.

"What're you doing for dinner?"

She rolled her eyes. "How am I supposed to know?"

Steeg got to his feet. "We'll do some Ethiopian tonight."

At least once a week they ate at a different ethnic restaurant. It served two purposes: a night out and a combination geography and history lesson. It was part of Steeg's life plan for DeeDee.

"We did that last week and it sucked, I had the rice with flies. 'Member?"

He laughed. "Okay, then, Turkish. See you later."

He waited until she was safely aboard the bus before he walked over to Dman.

CHAPTER FOUR

Feeney's was the most rare of rarities, a Prohibition speakeasy that had made it intact into the twenty-first century. The kind of a place where napkins didn't come with the drinks, and the owner didn't come to your table to ask if you were enjoying yourself. During Prohibition, Hell's Kitchen had more speakeasies than food stores, and Feeney's was the place where the lowlife elite congregated. Mobsters ranging from Al Capone to Meyer Lansky hoisted more than a few under Feeney's tin ceiling. Tucked between a T-shirt shop and a loading dock on Thirty-eighth and Twelfth, a block from the river, Feeney's was once a favorite haunt of Owney "The Killer" Madden, a mobster who ran Hell's Kitchen in the 1920s. Neighborhood lore had it that it was Madden and not Arnold Rothstein who'd fixed the 1919 World Series between the Chicago White Sox and the Cincinnati Reds. Steeg had no reason to doubt it.

After Prohibition it had hung on as a saloon. Now, a few old-timers stood at the mahogany bar doing shots and beer, listening to a Wurlitzer that played only John McCormack, Arthur Tracy, and The Chieftains. The fact that the owner was one Nick D'Amico, a small-time bookmaker and Columbo Family associate, didn't really matter.

Sipping on a mug of Guinness Stout, Steeg's older brother Dave, wearing a finely tailored navy blue suit, freshly starched white shirt, and a red-and-white-striped Windsor-knotted tie, sat in a back booth. Dave's theory was that business was serious and that you had to dress well to be taken seriously.

He wasn't alone.

Next to him sat Terry Sloan, similarly decked out in a snappy blue suit, silk tie, and slicked-back hair. He and Dave appeared to be deep in conversation. Sloan, a Hell's Kitchen's councilman, one of fifty-one wannabe power brokers with an eye on a congressional seat, was a local boy who had made good. He and Dave went way back. Steeg hadn't seen Sloan in some time, and didn't regret it. Maybe it was because he always treated him like Dave's pain-in-the-ass kid brother, or maybe he was just too slippery for Steeg's tastes. He wondered what Dave saw in him. Hanging out with lightweights, no matter how far back they went, just wasn't Dave's style.

Steeg slid in opposite them.

Dave hadn't lived in Hell's Kitchen since the break-up of the Westies, a particularly vicious gang of killers specializing in robbery, murder, and dismemberment. Once a charter member, Dave now preferred the bucolic atmosphere of Englewood Cliffs, just across the river in New Jersey. How Dave had escaped prison was something Steeg had never figured out. But Feeney's was still his office, the place where he did business.

And his business was something Steeg and Dave never discussed.

Sloan thrust out his hand. "How ya doin', Jack?"

Steeg took his hand. It was soft, like it hadn't seen real work in a very long time. "Pretty good. Am I interrupting?"

Sloan got to his feet. "Just leaving. I heard about what happened, y'know the suspension and all. Let me know if I can help. You know how it goes." He winked. "Us neighborhood guys gotta look after each other."

Steeg shook his head. "Everything's hunky-dory. Nothing I can't handle."

"Okay," Sloan said. "I'm outta here. See you around, Dave."

Dave waited until Sloan was gone before he pulled a cigar from his breast pocket and struck the flame of a Zippo to its tip. "Asshole," he said.

"What's he want?"

"What doesn't he want?"

"I thought you two were buddies."

"You're my buddy, and we're stuck with each other. Us against the world, just like always."

Steeg flapped his hand at the haze of blue smoke that hung above the table. "I thought smoking in bars was illegal now."

Dave shrugged. "This mayor doesn't smoke, so nobody's supposed to. The guy before him cheated on his wife and then closed down the porn shops. Where's it gonna end? Ah, screw all the politicians. They make guys like me look like altar boys. Enough about them. How's it going, Jakey?"

It would be hard to take them for brothers. Dave's close-cropped black hair was going to gray. And his wide shoulders, sprouting long arms with longshoreman's bunchy muscles, sat atop a massive chest. Dave was the defensive lineman to Steeg's wide receiver.

"Couldn't be better," Steeg replied.

"Off these, too?" Dave said, sliding a Cuban across the table.

Steeg slid it back. "Getting rid of bad habits."

"Hey, Nick," Dave shouted at the owner. "Two black coffees and a couple of Danish. Cheese. Make a fresh pot."

"How's Franny and the kids?"

"Good. They miss their uncle Jake. It's been a while."

"Yeah, well, I've been kind of busy."

"Really? Last time I checked, busy is the last thing you were. How're you holdin' up?"

"I don't like being screwed with. The guy Petrovitch smacked around was my informant. He was about to give me a one-man crime wave, a fucking serial rapist, but after being touched up by the Polack, my CI suddenly developed an acute case of amnesia."

"My offer still stands. I can fix it."

Steeg knew Dave could, but he didn't want that kind of help. "Thanks for the offer, but I'll pass."

"Whatever." He shrugged. "By the way, I ran into Ginny the other day. Shopping at Di Pietro's."

"Best cappicola in the city."

"Nice lady. Married now. A fireman. Lives somewhere at the end of the Long Island Expressway, out by exit 2000 or some shit like that. Y'know, civil service country. Anyway, she asked for you."

"That's good to know."

His ex-wife was someone Steeg didn't like to discuss, even with his brother. That she had remarried was mildly depressing news.

"It's funny how things work out, isn't it?"

"How's that?"

"I mean you were dating her since you had your first wet dream, then you marry her, and the first thing you want to do is get out of the Kitchen. She don't want to go, so *you* split."

"Is there a problem in there somewhere?"

"Well, here we are a couple of years later and she's out in the burbs and you're still here. What am I missing?"

Steeg still hadn't figured that one out yet. He and Ginny had married young. He was just out of the marines and enrolled at City College. She was nineteen, a bookkeeper at an import-export firm near the Battery. Not quite childhood sweethearts, but close. She wanted to be close to her family, and he wanted to get far away from his. He gave in and joined the police force and she was happy. His father wasn't.

Dominic Steeg wanted more than the cops for his son, something in an office. So did Steeg, but he went with the program. He and Ginny moved into a one-bedroom walk-up, where they drank wine on the fire escape and made love with the windows open while the breeze from the river cooled their naked bodies. It kind of worked for nine years. Ginny was happy with what was. He wasn't. Their divorce was his second strike on

Dominic's scorecard. Catholics don't do divorce. The recent suspension made three, and as far as Dominic was concerned, three was the charm. Since the divorce there had been other women, but nothing took. They went on to the rest of their lives, and he remained stuck in his.

"Let's just say it was a marriage of inconvenience," Steeg said, closing another chapter in his life.

Dave knew that he had overstepped and switched subjects. "Seen the old man lately?"

"No, but I did see Elvis in Times Square."

"C'mon, Jakey. Ever since Mom died, he's gone downhill. This is gonna sound strange comin' from me, but you gotta feel sorry for the miserable old bastard. I turned out to be a bum, but you were the good son."

"All the old man wanted was to bat a thousand, and he wound up hitting five hundred. Tough shit."

"I guess Pop should be happy. After all, Ted Williams only hit a bit over four," Dave said.

"Yeah, but in the kid department, he was oh for two. When Ted died, his son had his head separated from his body and had it freeze-dried, remember? Look, deep down, Dominic always figured I was no good, and now it's a self-fulfilling prophecy."

Dave reached across the table and gave Steeg's shoulder an affectionate squeeze. "C'mon, Jakey. I thought I was the only one in the family to hold a grudge."

Given Steeg's deepening malaise over the state of his life, he was sensitive to the implicit criticism buried in the compliment.

"That's crap! Grudge is my middle name. Remember Bobby Malone? About five years older than me."

"Yeah, short, mean little fuck. Never liked him. I banged his sister, though. She was a short, mean little fuck, too. What about him?"

"I guess I was nine or ten, and he scored some beer from Loscuito's Deli on Forty-fourth Street."

"Yeah, I know the place. Ran numbers out of the back. Good earner."

"Right. Anyway, he's standing with a bunch of his miscreant friends and he calls me over. Like, I'm flattered by the attention. I mean, he's a teenager and all. Anyway, he and his buddies are acting all friendly like, and he passes a bottle of beer to me. How could I say no. They're all big kids and they're making me feel like one of them. So I take a swig. The only thing is, it doesn't taste like the Rheingold we used to score from Dominic's when he was working. It was warm and flat and tasted like piss. Which, as it turned out, it was. Bobby thought it was the funniest thing he ever saw."

Dave's blue eyes turned glacial. It was a look that was hard to ignore, especially when you were on the receiving end, and Steeg was grateful he wasn't. Lots of scary mayhem usually followed. As a kid, Steeg practiced "the look" for hours in front of the mirror, but never got it quite right. He tried to emulate Dave's peculiar hitch-and-roll walk too, but gave it up when he realized that instead of tough, he looked constipated. "Why didn't you tell me?" he said, running his fingers lightly over his scarred cheek.

The scar, more a patch of whitish, pebbly skin, was the result of a dermabrasion and a laser procedure designed to erase a congenital port-wine stain from his cheek. As if being the son of a cop in this neighborhood wasn't enough to single Dave out for special treatment as a kid, the port-wine stain had cinched the deal. Dave, or "Red," as he was tagged, endured a uniquely vicious childhood. On his tenth birthday he'd decided he had had enough. The kid, a teenager who first labeled Dave with the nickname, had an unfortunate accident. Somehow he fell off of a roof. No one ever dared call Dave "Red" again, at least not to his face.

"'Cause I was going to handle it."

"What'd you do?"

"I followed him for days, waiting for the right time. Then, one night I caught him coming out of a skin flick in Times Square. I whacked him in the face with a baseball bat. Never had any problems after that."

D'amico brought their coffee and went back behind the bar.

Dave smiled. "How's the battle of the booze goin'?"

"I'm good today. Tomorrow is another story."

"Okay. Listen, the reason I mentioned the old man is because I saw this."

He passed a copy of the *New York Daily News* across the table. There, on the front page, was a picture of the dead woman during better times.

Steeg picked it up. "Holy shit! It's her."

"Name's Diana Strickland. I think maybe you ought to start thinking of trading up to a better neighborhood."

Steeg turned the page for the story.

"Anyway," Dave continued. "She's a dead ringer for her mother. I think her name was Lois, or Loretta, or something like that. Society broad. Disappeared years ago."

Steeg stopped reading. "What's one thing got to do with another?"

"I dunno. It just seems to be a hell of a coincidence, and you know how I feel about coincidences."

"What's the old man got to do with this?"

"It was his case."

It was all the incentive Steeg needed.

CHAPTER FIVE

Steeg didn't believe in the vagaries of Fate, the hand of Providence, the possibility of redemption, or coincidences. But this one was a doozie. Under normal circumstances he would have pulled the file up from the police department's database and learned all he needed to know about the missing Mrs. Strickland. But these weren't normal circumstances. Luce would help if he asked, but somehow Braddock would find out, putting her higher on his shit list. His father was a possibility, but that was a last resort. Why fuck up the rest of the day? That left the New York Public Library on Fifth at Forty-second Street.

He decided to walk. Cabs were for tourists or those flush with cash, and Steeg didn't fit in either category. He stopped at several payphones until he found one that worked, and dialed Luce's cell phone just to say hello. Most cops avoided him like a sexually transmitted disease, but not Luce. She was busy-up — to her elbows in gore, as she put it — so the conversation was short, but she did give him the names of the detectives who were working the case. Lou Gangemi, playing out his string until his pension kicked in, and Ray Swartz, supporting a wife, a girlfriend, three kids, and OTB. Both had a hard time detecting their asses with both hands. With these two jokers running the show, the case was heading into the cold-case files, a euphemism for the crapper.

Although he wasn't far from the library, on a whim Steeg decided to backtrack and see Herkie on the off chance that he might have seen or heard something the night of the murder. Given Herkie's usual anesthetized state, the chances were slim, but Steeg was hungry and it was an excuse to grab a slice from Sal's on Forty-eighth and Tenth. Thin crust, light on the tomato sauce, heavy on the cheese. The best pizza in the city.

Herkie's residence was an oversized carton set against a Dumpster in the lee of the wind. Herkie was in. A dirty white sweat sock attached to a foot poked out of the carton flap.

Steeg nodded approvingly. Herkie still had some brain cells intact. His shoes were his pillow, and few would be foolhardy or desperate enough to go in after them.

With the flat of his hand, Steeg hit the side of the carton, not hard enough to topple it but with just enough juice to get Herkie's attention. It was their daily ritual intended to make sure that Herkie was still among the living.

"Herkie, my man, it's Steeg. Rise and shine and greet another shitty day in the Big Apple."

Steeg waited for a response. A few minutes passed. Steeg raised his hand for another go at the carton. It usually took two or three good smacks to get Herkie off his butt.

Wearing the industrial padding like a toga, Herkie

stumbled from the carton. From the looks of him, he hadn't spent a restful night. His eyes were red-rimmed and glassy, a week-old growth of gray stubble sprouting from his cheeks.

"Enough, already! As you can plainly see, I'm still drawing breath, and more's the pity," he said. "If I had the balls, I'd throw myself into the river and leave this vale of tears."

"What's stopping you?" This conversation was part of their daily routine.

"I can't swim."

Different day, same line, but Steeg chuckled nevertheless. Herkie expected it.

"You don't look so hot."

"Neither do you, hotshot."

"I know shelters are out, but just say the word and you're into a nice, warm, treatment facility. Three hots and a cot."

Herkie took a long moment to survey the street. "What, and miss out on all this? And since when did you become a fucking social worker?"

Steeg let it slide. There were so many Herkies to contend with—belligerent, whiney, mellow, sly, wheedling, schizoid—he never knew on any day which one would show up. Now that he knew, he got down to business.

"You heard about the girl they found dead in my building?" With Herkie, you had to deal with the big picture before you got down to specifics. If that didn't work, you were out of luck.

"Fucking sirens woke me up. You cops just can't let sleeping junkies lie."

"So that's it, huh."

"No, this is."

He stood straight up and wrapped his makeshift toga tightly around his body. Suddenly, the expression on his face changed, and his eyes took on a faraway look as if reaching back to a distant time of dignity and pride. In an uncharacteristically strong, steady voice he declaimed:

Oh! we, who have known shame, we have found
    release there,
        Where there's no ill, no grief, but sleep has mending,
            Naught broken save this body, lost but breath;
Nothing to shake the laughing heart's long peace there
        But only agony, and that has ending;
            And the worst friend and enemy is but Death.

Herkie was in rare form.

"In case you're wondering, that was Rupert Brooke. One of his war sonnets. Now," he said, returning to his carton, "Here comes an original Herkie. Been working on it for some time. You know, to get it just right, so you could get my meaning without the slightest bit of ambiguity." He paused for effect. "Fuck off!"

"I have to hand it to you, Herkie. Old Rupert could have learned a lot from you. No wasted words."

Smiling, Steeg reached into his pocket and withdrew a ten-dollar bill and tossed it into the carton, hoping that Herkie would spend it on food but knowing that he wouldn't. He'd stopped making moral judgments a long time ago. For better or worse, people did what they did and that was just the way things were.

He walked east on Forty-eighth Street toward Fifth. The post-Thanksgiving gridlock was in full swing, and the air reeked of boiling hot dogs and car exhaust. Zigzagging through the streets to make time against the heavy traffic, he passed his alma mater, the parochial school of the Church of the Precious Blood, on Forty-third near Ninth. Even now it gave him the willies. When the priest-abuse scandals broke, Steeg wasn't surprised. He didn't know—no one ever talked—but he knew. And the memory of the Holy Justice regularly administered by the ageless but fierce Sister Mary Domenica, the resident dominatrix, was enough to make him start bedwetting again. With uncanny ability bordering on the mystic, she could read the current and future sins of her charges with frightening accuracy. Sister Mary Dominica's sole message to her band of miscreants, underachievers, and incubating criminals was stark and simple: If the call to Holy Orders didn't come, there were only two life destinations available — a job with the City, or prison.

Sister Mary Domenica wasn't big on expanding horizons.

Food on the table, shelter from the wind, and a few bucks coming in—but not enough to indulge one's basest passions — was more her speed. But the good Sister did have one thing right, though. The library was the one place the bastards couldn't hurt you. And to those precious few of her students with an interest in learning, everything one ever wanted to know about anything was to be found there. For Steeg, the library was sanctuary, the place to go when his father came off shift.

Steeg found an empty computer terminal and Googled Diana Strickland. Apparently the name was common, and for some reason he couldn't figure out why her half dozen or so namesakes felt compelled to post their own Web pages, filling them with chatty family histories, prom photos, and annoying prose. The problem was that these Diana Stricklands lived in places like Fargo and Kissimmee and Bemidji. If there was nothing on the daughter, without the benefit of a first name, how was he going to find her mother? He moved away from the terminal and walked to the desk. Dave had said that his father had worked the mother's case and that she was a society lady. Surely her death would have hit the tabloids, if not the *Times*. As a library regular, Steeg had no problem getting permission to access the library's microfiche newspaper file. Now he had to narrow his search down. His father's years of service on the force was a good place to begin.

After serving in the infantry during the Korean War, Dominic Steeg had drifted through a succession of dead-end jobs before joining the police force on April 1, 1958. Shortly after, he married Brooklyn's own Norah Dowd. The words from "Poem for Erika-For Baby," a Peter, Paul and Mary song, always came to mind when he thought of her. "The leaves will bow down when you walk by." Why she married Dominic eluded Steeg.

Dave took her death especially hard. Steeg always

suspected it had something to do with the port-wine stain. For some cockeyed reason, Dominic, never religious, was somehow convinced that Dave's very visible defect was a punishment from God for some unspecified sin, and he never let Dave forget it. Norah, religious to the core, thought that Dominic was full of shit; infants weren't capable of sin. The lines were drawn and remained that way until her too-early death. Ten years after joining the force, Dominic was promoted to Detective. So, 1968 seemed like a likely place to begin his search. Two hours later he found what he was looking for on page three of the August 6, 1975, edition of the *Daily News*.

The headline screamed in thirty-six-point type:

Blue Blood Stains Fifth Avenue Socialite Slain

Catchy, Steeg thought, perusing the article. Long on lurid details, the story was short on facts. Linda — not Lois or Loretta, as Dave had recalled–Strickland, the wife of Earl Strickland, a major player on Wall Street and heir to the Strickland Publishing fortune, was pushed or fell from her Fifth Avenue penthouse apartment. In addition to her husband, two daughters, eight-year-old Caroline and four-year-old Diana, survived her. There were no signs of forced entry. When questioned about possible suspects, Detectives Dominic Steeg and Ted Maggiore issued terse no comments. The Stricklands were heavy hitters in New York society. There had been Stricklands in New York since the British booted the Dutch out of New Amsterdam.

Steeg followed the story until the press lost interest three days after her death. It was about right. Three days was the typical half-life of a celebrity murder/suicide. All in all, her death was pretty straightforward stuff, and that was the problem. The late Mrs. Strickland hadn't been despondent. Not under a doctor's care. No history of emotional problems. She'd loved her husband and children. A regular pillar of the community.

According to the newspaper accounts, the doorman on duty saw and heard nothing. The same for the neigbors. Not unusual in a building like Steeg's, where the Son of Sam could be picking off people with a handgun and no one would think it was out of the ordinary, but a bit strange in a building whose tenants would complain to high heaven if someone so much as laughed out loud. To top it all off, this was a high-profile case, and the Stricklands were politically connected. Normally the Department would have turned itself inside out to find the bad guy, if there was one. Steeg spent the rest of the afternoon combing every New York City newspaper up to the present to see if it had. Apparently, it hadn't. The facts, if that's what they were, simply didn't make sense.

He heard the urgent whisper. *Walk away!*

Easier said than done.

CHAPTER SIX

The Ankara, at Thirty-ninth and Tenth, was your basic Hell's Kitchen restaurant: pretty good food, low prices, and far enough away from the Theater District to get a table at 7:00. Besides, the restaurant was heavy on ambience, something to interest DeeDee; intricately patterned rugs on the floor, lots of brass, waiters wearing bloused white shirts and black pants cinched with red sashes at the waist, and piped-in dirge-like music for Steeg.

Steeg ordered for both of them. Manti, dumplings of dough filled with meat and served with yogurt. Cheese-filled borek, and rice pilaf with onions, tomatoes, and green peppers sautéed in butter and garlic. And two Cokes with cherries to wash it all down.

"How was your day?"

"Fine," DeeDee said, unmoved by the ambience.

"How was school?"

"Fine."

He was running out of questions faster than she was running out of monosyllabic answers.

"Did you study up on Turkey?"

"Yeah," she said, in a distracted sort of way.

Steeg wondered what the problem was but plowed on, anyway.

"Okay, where is it?"

"Near Queens," she said, chewing on a fingernail.

It was going to be one of those evenings, he thought, deciding to save the geography lesson for another time.

Their food arrived, and she played with it, moving bits of rice around like they were chess pieces.

"Good, huh?"

"It's all right."

He pushed his plate away and leaned his elbows on the table. "Okay, what's bothering you?"

She plucked the cherry from the Coke and popped it into her mouth, chewing on it while trying to frame her question. After a few moments, she had it. "Do you believe in God, Steeg?"

The question startled him. "Do you?"

"I asked you first."

The simple answer was no. Sister Mary Domenica had cured him of that. In Steeg's theology, God was a delusion created by men to give them a reason to wake up in the morning to a world filled with evil. If there was a God, He was on holiday. But could he tell her that? If he didn't, her built-in bullshit meter would sound the alarm, shredding whatever trust he had built up over the past few months.

"No, I don't."

"Me neither," she responded, finally meeting his gaze.

"Why'd you ask?"

Her eyes filled with tears. "I miss my mother so much, it hurts."

He reached over and cradled her face in his hands. "I know you do, and I wish there was something I could do about it."

"You're trying, Steeg, I know you are."

Steeg thought of his own mother and knew exactly how she felt. It was time to lighten the mood. "Want to see a trick?"

"Sure."

He plucked the stem from the cherry and popped it in his mouth. "Watch this."

Steeg's lips and tongue moved into action, contorting his face into something resembling a bout of Tourette's sydrome.

DeeDee giggled. "You look like you're having a stroke."

In twenty seconds he parted his lips and stuck out his tongue. On its tip lay the cherry stem, perfectly knotted in the middle.

"Ta-da," he said, holding it up for her inspection.

"Holy shit!" she exclaimed, grinning. "With a talent like that, how come you don't date very much?"

He let her comment pass; at least he'd got her smiling again.

"Want to see me go for the world record, the never-attempted sheepshank with a double-bow hitch?"

Before she could answer, Steeg saw Terry Sloan and a tall black man with a graying beard stroll into the restaurant. Politics, indeed, made strange bedfellows, Steeg thought.

Anytime Gideon El made an appearance, he drew attention. Garbed in a flowing dashiki, a silver-embroidered red skullcap, and a combination Star of David and crucifix hanging from a chain as wide around as a fire hose, Gideon El, nee Randall Carver, cut quite a figure. Steeg remembered him as a small-time hustler with a big-time rap sheet who realized that there was a lot more money to be made in racial activism than three-card monte.

Carver's game was a variation of the old protection racket. He would target a business, trump up some discrimination, and threaten to close it down unless the owners hired a token black or Hispanic and made regular and sizable contributions to Carver's Freedom League. When things went bad, which they sometimes did, Carver sat back while a couple of his followers took the fall. Steeg recalled one of Carver's protests at a Bronx shoe store that went very bad. After a week of picketing, one of Carver's crazies decided to take matters into his own hands. He torched the store, killing the proprietor and three employees, all black. Carver shed some public crocodile tears, blaming the tragedy on rampant racism, and moved on to his next payday while the arsonist took the fall. Steeg had very real problems with Randall Carver.

Sloan reddened when he noticed Steeg. Quickly recovering, he donned his politician's smile and walked over to Steeg's table. Gideon El wasn't far behind.

"I haven't seen you in a couple of years, and now it's twice in one day. We gotta stop meeting like this, people are gonna talk," he said, delivering a jab-in-the-ribs wink. "What brings you here, Jake?"

Steeg managed a tight smile. "Good company" — he nodded to DeeDee — "and good food, and now they're both ruined. DeeDee, this is Councilman Terry Sloan. He's an important man in this city. And" — he pointed to Gideon El — "this other gentleman is Randall Carver, and he isn't."

Sloan had had more than enough of Steeg for one day. "God damn it, why do you have to be such a pain in the ass all the time?"

"It's genetic, as a quick gander at the Steeg family tree will reveal." He held up his hand and used his fingers as bullet points. "Let's see, you got your Irish. Major assholes, especially when they're drinking, or Brits are around, or other Irishmen, actually. Then you got your Vikings. We all know they had a hard time playing nicely with others. Always pissed off those Norsemen, but fun at a party. Drank mead out of human skulls. Then, you got your Germans, who gave us the Holocaust. A real fun-loving bunch. Do you know anyone who wants to spend five minutes with a Kraut? And you're surprised I am the way I am?"

"Thanks for the swing through the branches — what's your problem with Gideon?"

Steeg turned his attention from Sloan and leveled it at Gideon El. "I don't have much use for somebody who stokes the dreams of people who believe he's going lead them across the river to the Promised Land and leaves them sitting on the bank while he hops the boat."

Steeg pointed to the metal contraption hanging from his neck and continued. "On to your next new thing, Randall? Gonna bring Jews and Christians together in peace and harmony? Everybody sitting around singing 'Kumbaya' while you got your hand in their pockets?"

Unabashed, Carver allowed himself a small smile. "We've never met, have we, and yet you dislike me."

Sloan took Carver's arm. "Let's get out of here."

Carver shrugged Sloan's hand away. "Just one moment." He turned to Steeg. "Randall Carver is a man I used to be, but I understand that you have problems of your own, ex-Detective Steeg. You see, I know all about you, too, sir."

"Then you know that kissing your ass like everybody else in this city isn't part of my job description anymore. Now, I'm going to have dinner and I suggest you do the same."

"You're a prick, you know that, Jack?" Sloan hissed.

"Yeah, but I at least know who my friends are, Terry." He turned back to DeeDee. "Now, where were we?"

"In Asia Minor, right in the middle of Georgia, Armenia, Syria, Iraq, Iran, Bulgaria, and Greece."

"What?"

She shot him a sly smile. "Turkey. You asked where it was. 'Member?"

CHAPTER SEVEN

Steeg stood outside his father's apartment house on Fifty-third and Eighth, waiting for Luce. The message left on his answering machine the night before said that she wanted to fill him in on the investigation into Diana Strickland's murder. Luce knew Steeg well enough to know that idleness was not his long suit, and this was her way of keeping him involved. The truth was, and he didn't have the heart to tell her, that he was far more interested in Diana's mother's death. And that's why he was stamping life back into his freezing feet trying to muster the energy to pay Dominic a visit.

Steeg checked his watch. Ten fifteen a.m. Luce was late. He pulled the watch cap down over his ears and buttoned his canvas jacket up to the neck. The wind ripped through his jeans like a fusillade of buckshot.

The block he had grown up on had changed. Cute little restaurants and trendy boutiques had replaced candy stores, head shops, and XXX movie theaters. Even the people looked different, like they had just stepped out of an Eddie Bauer catalog. The Kitchen was succumbing to gentrified crawl, and the urban pioneers with their fancy little dogs and Thinsulate coats were winning.

A car pulled up beside him, and the passenger-side window slid down.

"Hey, Jackson!" Luce called, motioning for him to get in. "You look like a panhandler. Get in out of the cold."

Steeg opened the door of the unmarked Ford sedan and slid in next to her. The warmth felt good.

"You're shiverin'," she said, grabbing his hands and vigorously massaging his fingers. "How come you don't wear gloves?"

"Not manly." He paused between chill spasms. "You're late."

He gazed at the multicolored cocoon she had wrapped around her. A maize yellow knit hat pulled over her ears and down to her eyebrows. A red-and-white-striped scarf coiled around her neck pulled up to her chin. A dark gray bordering on blue coat with moss green patches at the armpits. Knee-high boots and gloves completed the ensemble. "Nice outfit. The scarf is a particularly interesting touch. Makes you look like a barber pole."

She passed him a steaming container of coffee. "Here, it's Kona blended with some Colombian roast picked from the south side of the mountain, where it gets the perfect combination of sunlight and humidity. Time they pick 'em, those beans about to burst. I found this place in the Village, where couriers mule this stuff in daily so you get the perfect degree of flavor. One day too early or too late and the magic is gone. Drink it, it'll put some zing in your get-go, mon."

He wrapped his hands around the container, feeling

the heat seep into his joints. "Don't tell me you believe that shit."

"What shit?"

"South side of the mountain. Humidity. You sound like one of those oenophiles who go ga-ga over the grapes, like how many feet stomped it into a paste, the wood the casks are made from. The whole nine yards."

She rolled her eyes. "Just drink it and tell me if I'm wrong."

He took a sip, scalding his tongue. "I like Dunkin' Donuts's better."

"Did anyone ever tell you you're a mood killer, Steeg?"

"All the time."

"So, what's going on?"

"It's wonderful to have time on your hands. Thought maybe I'd play tourist. You know, take the ferry out to the Statue of Liberty, ride to the top of the Empire State Building, maybe take a walking tour of the hidden New York."

"Why don't you?"

"Would you?"

"Nah. Too dangerous. You know, before I was a cop, I wouldn't think twice about it, but now that I know there are bad guys just waiting to slice and dice me and take my money, I have no interest."

"My sentiments exactly. So, I decided to drop in on my father."

"Uh-oh. When was the last time you saw him?"

Steeg took another sip of coffee and made a face.

"Unlike wine, this doesn't get better with age." He

set the cup down on the dashboard. "I guess it was Dave's daughter's First Communion. He wouldn't walk into the church, so he stood at the doorway."

"He's got problems with the Church?"

"Who doesn't? Nah, problems with Dave, his first disappointment. What have you got for me?"

"Not a lot. The deceased apparently came from a lot of money. The technical term is 'shitload.' Her father's a retired stockbroker. They live up on Fifth Avenue. There's an older sister in the picture. Nobody's talking. The M.E.'s report isn't in yet, and we don't have a line on Moore, the tenant."

"Sounds like Gangemi and Swartz have it all figured out."

"Mutt and Jeff? Yeah, they're up to their old tricks."

"Listen, I need a favor."

"Just name it."

"About twenty-five years ago, Diana's mother was killed."

"That's a hell of a 'ting. This job never surprises."

"Yeah. Anyway, I need the file."

Luce's eyes narrowed. "Why?"

"I'm intrigued, let's leave it at that."

"Do you think there might be a connection?"

"If there is, you'll be the first to know."

"I'll see what I can do." She checked her watch. "I'm out of here. Oh, the Strickland family is having a memorial service for the girl. Tomorrow, at Cropsey's. Nine a.m."

"But the M.E. hasn't released the body."

"Yeah, the burial is going to be private whenever

he's done, somewhere in Westchester. I guess they figured the ceremony could be held anytime. Dead is dead, right?"

Dead is dead, Steeg agreed.

Dominic Steeg looked like he hadn't shaved in weeks. His eyes were red-rimmed and his skin was a jaundiced yellow. Although he didn't smell of alcohol, Steeg suspected he was drinking again. The family curse, handed down through the generations like a treasured heirloom.

The apartment hadn't changed since the last time he was there, over a year before. The same familiar smell of his mother's perfume. Shalimar. The same overstuffed furniture with doilies, "antimacassars" she called them. Very lace curtain and neat as a pin.

Dominic parked himself in his Barcalounger positioned in front of the TV set and stared at two ESPN commentators nattering on about the Giants' losing season.

"What do you want?" Dominic said, never taking his eyes off the screen.

"How're you doing?"

"Since when do you give a shit?"

This is going well, Steeg thought.

"Giants never should have gotten rid of Collins," Steeg said. "The new guy looks like a teenager, and Tiki Barber couldn't hold the ball if it was welded to his hands. You think Dayne's gonna get a shot?"

Dominic flashed Steeg a sour look. "Are we supposed to be bonding here? You know, prodigal son returns and bullshits about nothing and works his way up to asking for forgiveness. But that's not in your nature, is it?"

"Forgiveness for what?" Steeg said.

"Screwing up your career, for starters. Ginny was right to leave you. Misery follows you like a bad smell."

"It never changes, does it? Can we leave my ex-wife out of this? If you've got something to say to me, say it."

Dominic waved his hand in disgust. "Whatever."

"Pop, I'm sorry Mom died. I'm sorry I'm not Chief of Detectives. I'm sorry John Kennedy got shot. I'm sorry I haven't hit the Lotto yet, and I'm really sorry I'm not the son you figured I'd be, but sometimes stuff happens." He rapped his fist against his chest, hard. "Mea culpa. Mea maxima culpa."

"You were the one I was banking on, and you covered yourself with shame. You covered this whole family with shame."

This is getting old, Steeg thought. "Pop, I wasn't on the take, I just slugged someone who needed it."

At the commercial break, Dominic surfed through the channels, finally settling on an old John Wayne movie. *Sands of Iwo Jima.*

Perfect, Steeg thought. "I have a question."

"Shoot."

An inviting proposition.

Steeg walked over and positioned himself between Dominic and the TV set. "A woman was found dead in my apartment building. Strickland. Diana Strickland."

It was almost imperceptible, but Steeg saw his father stiffen.

"Anyway," he continued, "turns out that she was the daughter of Linda Strickland. You might remember the case."

"You're in my way."

Steeg held his position. "It was your case, wasn't it?"

"It was a long time ago. Besides, what's it to you, you ain't on the job anymore."

"Call it professional interest. What can you tell me about it?"

"There's nothing to tell. Happened a long time ago."

"How did she die?"

Dominic Steeg's gaze drifted to the window.

"Murder, suicide, never figured it out."

"Dead is dead, right?"

"Dead is dead," Dominic agreed.

It wasn't until Steeg was in the street that he realized that he had made an incorrect assumption. Dominic hadn't been drinking, he'd been crying.

CHAPTER EIGHT

Steeg swapped his jeans and work boots for a navy blue suit, dark patterned tie, and black lace-up shoes and arrived at Cropsey's half an hour before the memorial service began. He spotted Gangemi and Swartz sitting in their unmarked eating breakfast. The front seat bore a striking resemblance to a McDonald's trash bin.

He rapped his knuckles against the window. "Lou, Ray. How're you boys doing?"

Swartz was so startled that he dropped his bagel with cream cheese and jelly facedown on the Racing Form spread out on his lap.

"God damn it!" he yelled. "What the fuck!"

"What are the odds on that, Ray? You know, you flip a coin a hundred times and the law of probability says each flip is a singular occurrence unrelated to the other flips. So, you got a fifty-fifty chance of heads or tails. But with bagels it always works out jam side down. It's a puzzlement. Matzoh works that way, too. Could it be a Jewish thing?"

Gangemi rolled the window down. "What are you doing here?"

"I'm with the groom," Steeg deadpanned.

"Very funny," Swartz said, scraping the jelly off the Gulfstream results with a napkin. "You're a very funny guy."

"If you're willing to spring for the cover, I'll be appearing at The Comedy Store this weekend. But enough of this witty banter. I guess I'll see you guys inside. Oh, in case you haven't figured it out, the entrance is on Broadway. Anything to help our boys in blue. Ta-ta!"

"Dickwad!" Gangemi said.

"Asshole!" Swarz agreed.

Thomas A. Cropsey Funeral Home was a New York institution, the final stop for New York's great and not quite great. It was decorated in dark somber colors, thick carpets, and muted, recessed lighting. Mantovani elevator music played softly in the background. Consolation Counselors—no Funeral Directors here—patrolled the premises in gray Brooks Brothers suits. Each one looked like he had a Harvard MBA. The overall effect was that of a restricted WASP club where death was not only unacknowledged, it was a word never spoken lest it offend.

In the foyer, Steeg signed the guest register and a Harvard MBA directed him to the Remembrance Room. Although the room was barely filled, he took a seat in the last row and settled back to watch the guests parade in. He didn't have long to wait before the cream of New York's power elite made their appearance. Many he didn't recognize, but several he did. Apparently, there was a protocol of procession. First came the governor and the mayor waltzing down the center aisle, followed by an assortment of local and state politicians. Next, a sprinkling of men who looked like bankers and corporate heads wearing pale blue shirts with white collars, muted ties appropriate for the occasion, and expressions that said, "This better not last to too long or my whole day is going to be fucked." Then, a large group of young people Steeg assumed were friends of Diana's, and after that was catch as catch can. The big surprise was Councilman Terry Sloan walking arm in arm with Gideon El. One thing was clear: Strickland had more juice than anyone had a right to have.

The soft murmur of conversation ceased when the Reverend Ralph Jemison, the pastor of St. James Presbyterian, appeared from a side door and took his place at the raised lectern in front. Jemison, a celebrity in his own right, had his own weekly television show, and for the fifth week in a row his latest book, *God Loves Rich People, Too,* was number one on the *New York Times*'s nonfiction best-seller list. With an upward sweep of his arms he ordered everyone to rise. Mantovani swung into a Bach fugue, signaling the entrance of the bereaved family. Emerging from an open door in the back, Caroline Strickland appeared, standing behind a wheelchair containing the slumped form of her father, Earl. A gray-haired man in a dark suit stood next to her. Steeg noticed that Swartz and Gangemi had taken up positions against the far wall.

Earl Strickland appeared to have been suffering the effects of a stroke. The muscles in his face were slack, his eyes closed, and his once large frame seemed to have collapsed in on itself.

Caroline was entirely another story. Wearing no jewelry and a simple black dress, she was tall and fine-featured, with long auburn hair draped over a swan-like neck. The little makeup she wore was designed to look like she wore no makeup at all. Steeg was hard-pressed to believe that she and Diana were sisters. The gray-haired man wheeled her father to the front, positioned the chair in front of the first pew, and retreated. Caroline trailed behind, keeping a distance. She took a seat near her father but not next to him. There were no other family members present.

The Reverend Jemison made relatively short work of the ceremony. His theme was an elegy on the loss of innocence. Steeg thought it strange, especially since the good reverend didn't connect it to the details of Diana's life or death. It was a sermon completely in the air, rootless, ephemeral, and perfunctory. Too perfunctory. In fifteen minutes he was finished, and so was the service. No other eulogies, encomiums, or perorations. No tears.

Nothing.

As if glad to be done with the whole affair, Caroline rose and wheeled her father to the back and through the open door, a move that even made the good Reverend Jemison uncomfortable. With nothing else on the agenda, he, for the first time, invoked the name of the Deity.

"Go with God," he said, and disappeared through the door through which he had entered.

WASPS really are different Steeg, thought, reflecting on the grave-diving, tombstone–head banging, banshee-screaming funerals he fondly remembered. But he quickly chided himself for judging another's grief. When you got right down to it, there is no standard response to death.

He noticed a reception line forming and he hung back in his seat until the chapel had emptied. One thing was clear: There wasn't a lot of love in the room. Finally, he rose and joined the end of the line.

Caroline stood next to her father and accepted condolences delivered with air kisses and grim faces. Earl Strickland appeared to be sleeping. Under the soft light, Caroline's hair glinted with copper highlights.

Steeg noted the relief in her eyes when she saw that he was the last in line.

"I'm sorry for your loss," Steeg said.

"You're a cop, aren't you?" It was more a statement than a question.

Steeg wasn't about to correct her assumption of his official status within the police department. This wasn't the time for subtleties. "How did you make me?"

Her voice deepened. *"I'm sorry for your loss,"* she mimicked. "Do they teach you that in cop school?"

Steeg was nonplussed.

"You people simply have to come up with a different line. Over the past few days I've talked to everyone from Inspector down to Abbott and Costello over there." She jerked her chin in the direction of Swartz and Gangemi, who were helping themselves to coffee and a selection of Pepperidge Farm cookies laid out on silver platters.

"I don't know what more I can tell you."

"Oh. I was afraid you were going to say it was my cheap suit."

Her eyes momentarily sparkled with amusement. "That, too."

Steeg liked her immediately.

"Let's just say I have a personal interest. Your sister's body was found in my apartment building. I tend to take those things seriously. All I really want is a few minutes of your time."

Caroline considered this, appraising him as she did. Apparently, she liked what she saw.

"Okay," she said. "Lunch tomorrow. Noon. Le Morel, on Seventy-third. Do you know it?"

"Does it have tablecloths?"

"Would that matter?"

"Actually, yes."

"Think of it as a new experience."

"I'll dress casual."

With a mischievous smile, she rubbed his lapel between her thumb and forefinger.

"I insist."

CHAPTER NINE

Something was wrong, and Steeg couldn't put his finger on it. The street was empty. Not unusual for a winter day. In summer, the street roared with life. Dominoes, open fire hydrants, the smoke of roasting barbecue, the beat of rap and salsa, and rivers of beer. A natural order to things. The stars were aligned and everything was in perfect balance.

But even the dead time of winter had its own subtle symmetry, and now it was disturbed. It took Steeg a few seconds to realize that the imbalance was caused by Herkie's absence.

His flattened cardboard box sat in the middle of the street, and his books were strewn about like confetti. Ripped-off covers, torn-out pages. Few were intact. It had taken one cruel son of a bitch to do this, and it was enough to make Steeg sick. Hopkins, Joyce, Hemingway, Herkie's beloved War Poets, and so many others were turned into garbage.

Steeg prowled Forty-eighth Street collecting them, determined to catalog and replace each one and make the person who did it pay. He dropped them off in his apartment and went back outside. The street was still empty. A ship's horn broke the silence.

He went into Sal's Pizzeria. If anyone saw anything it was Sal Matarazzo, Forty-eighth Street's self-appointed watch patrol.

A beefy man with thick black hair and hands like a catcher's mitt, Sal was engrossed in beating a round of dough into the thickness of a transparency.

"What can I get for you, Steeg?" he said, without looking up.

"What happened to Herkie, Sal?"

"Fuck if I know."

"Don't give me that shit."

Sal slapped the dough on the marble counter. "I feed him every day." There was a whining, apologetic tone to his voice.

"So you're a philanthropist, but it doesn't answer the question."

Sal kept his eyes glued on the hunk of dough as if it were the repository of ancient mysteries waiting to be revealed. "I got a business here. People who depend on me."

"What are you saying, Sal."

"I'm saying I don't want trouble."

"You never were afraid of anybody. Remember Jimmy Dolan, ran with the Westies?"

A smile crept to his lips. "That was a long time ago."

"He owed you on a bet and you threw him in the pizza oven."

His smile grew wider. "Threw a hunk of mozzarella on him. Melted all over his silk shirt." His smile faded.

"That was a different time. You don't get it, Steeg. They're squeezing me. Can't get insurance. They tripled the rent. Pat is in college at thirty large a year. What do you want from me?"

"What happened to Herkie?"

He grabbed the dough and threw it against the wall.

"Shit! Okay, it was Dman and his crew. They're bad guys, Steeg. Not like we used to be. We had rules. They don't. There's something going on around here, and I don't know what it is. If you can figure it out, let me know."

"Thanks, Sal."

"Fuck thanks. You want a slice?"

"Is it going to come from that thing slithering down the wall over there?"

"Waste not, want not."

Steeg caught up to Dman lounging on a bench at De Witt Clinton Park on Twelfth Avenue, right across from where the *Queen Mary 2* had docked. Traffic was at a standstill. People had driven in from Long Island and Westchester to see the ship that was longer than the Chrysler Building was tall. Vendors were out in the street doing a brisk business in commemorative *Queen Mary* T-shirts. Dman appeared to be doing a brisk business too. At Steeg's approach, someone yelled, "Five Oh!" and his customers scattered like birds.

Dman leaned back, and his lips curled into a half-mocking smile.

That was all it took. Steeg's eyes glazed with a black mist.

He was in the grip of the vortex, trapped in a black

whirlwind of rage, spinning out of control, grasping wildly for something to hold on to or run the risk of being lost forever in the blackness. It was the reason he had quit drinking, believing that it was alcohol that had fueled his dark episodes. Moments like this reminded him of a truth he had a hard time acknowledging: He and Dave were cut from the same tattered cloth.

Steeg walked up to Dman and smacked him on the side of the head, sending him and his rose-tinted Oakleys sprawling.

"Yo!" Dman sputtered, looking up at Steeg looming over him. "'Sup with dat? Fuck you hittin' me?"

"That was for Herkie," he said. He drew back his foot and kicked Dman in the balls. "And this is because you piss me off."

A whooshing sound like air rushing from a balloon exploded from Dman's lips as he grabbed his crotch and curled into a ball.

Steeg reached down and grabbed a handful of sweatshirt and hauled him back on the bench.

"You fried, man. This is fuckin' police brutality. I'm gonna sue your white ass."

Steeg flashed him a malevolent grin. "Remember, I'm not a cop anymore, just a guy with a grudge and the disposition of a pit bull. Now, what happened to Herkie, numbnuts? Just so you know, I use that term literally."

Dman's hands remained cocooned around his balls. "Don't know what you're talkin' about. Don't know any Herkie, an' I don't want to know *you!*"

"Let me ask you a question. Where did you get the

tag 'Dman'? Is there a book of stupid nicknames you morons go to when you run out of ideas? Or could it be you're a golfer?" He paused. "Nah, it's gotta be the book of stupid names."

Dman stared at Steeg through uncomprehending eyes.

"One more time, Rahim. Why did you roust Herkie? An answer would be nice, or else I'm going to go another round with your nuts. And when I'm done, all your little dusty friends are going to be calling you 'Dgirl.' "

"He was fuckin' up the neighborhood."

Steeg was stunned.

"*He* was fucking up the neighborhood?"

"It's the troof."

"That is so staggeringly moronic, I honestly don't know how to respond."

Like a turtle retreating into its shell, Dman's head receded into his hood.

"It's the fuckin' troof," he repeated, his voice a weak echo beneath the folds of cloth.

"Stand up and empty your pockets."

"What?"

Steeg reached down, grabbed two handfuls of sweatshirt, and hauled him to his feet.

"What part of 'empty your pockets' didn't you understand? Lay everything on the bench."

Dman did as he was told. Out came a half dozen dime bags of crack, a thick roll of money, and a .25 caliber pistol with electrician's tape wrapped around the handle.

Steeg fingered the tape.

"Business must not be too good if all you can afford is this itty-bitty little thing."

Dman remained silent.

Steeg stuck the pistol in his pocket and swept the crack off the bench and ground it out under his shoe.

"I don't want to strain your brain, but pick up the money and count it," he said. "If I'm right, they're all fives and tens for the nickel and dime bags you're peddling."

Dman snatched the money up from the bench and totaled it up.

"Three hundred and seventy-five dollars."

"Give it here."

"Oh, man!" he said, reluctantly passing it to Steeg. "You're fuckin' robbin' me."

"Consider it a donation to the Herkie Book Fund."

"Damn!"

Tiny flakes of the umpteenth snowfall of the season swirled about.

"Did you hurt him?"

"Nah, just chased his ass. Told him to find some other street to shit on."

"Give me your shoes."

"Say what?"

"And while you're at it, throw in your socks. It's time to walk a mile in Herkie's shoes, or, in your case, lack of them."

"You gotta be shittin' me! It's fuckin' snowing."

Steeg grinned a malevolent grin. "Why is it you can't ever find a cop when you need one?"

CHAPTER TEN

Le Morel confirmed Steeg's worst fears. Acres of snow-white tablecloths. Cut flowers in slender crystal flutes. Goblets and glasses of varying sizes and shapes, and a fish knife at every place setting. It was a nightmare. As if that wasn't enough, the place looked like it was hosting an eating-disorder convention. Women wearing Chanel and Versace sipped Mojitos very carefully for fear that their skin would split if they moved their lips.

He gave Caroline's name to the Junior Leaguer doubling as the greeter who flashed him a stiff BOTOX smile. She motioned to a pre-BOTOX junior greeter with an armful of menus, who led him to Caroline's table.

Caroline wore a hooded Nile blue warm-up suit that was never intended to see the inside of a gym, but it set off her pale green eyes perfectly. Her hair was tied in a ponytail. A touch of lip gloss completed the picture. She looked glorious.

Caroline put down her drink and smiled. "Casual enough?"

Steeg took a seat next to her. The pre-BOTOX greeter handed him a menu and left.

"You or the restaurant?"

"Take your pick."

"You, hands down."

"You look better in slacks and a sweater than a suit. They seem to contain you better."

Her voice had a lyrical quality, mellow shadings of irony mixed with unadorned directness.

"Want something to drink?" she asked.

"A club soda would be fine."

"So, you're one of those."

"One of what?"

"A dieter, a gym rat, or a drunk. From the looks of you, my initial feeling would be gym rat, but my guts tell me drunk."

She signaled a waiter wearing enough gold piping on his jacket to pass for an imperial hussar. Very retro in a city where restaurant wait staff dressed like refugees from an NYU dorm room.

"Take this away," she said, handing him her drink. "And bring us two club sodas."

The waiter fish-eyed her. Club soda was so passé. "Sparkling water, perhaps, or Perrier?"

She leveled him with a stare. "Two *club* sodas."

"That was very thoughtful," Steeg said.

"No, just another human being trying to keep her balance on the high wire of life."

Steeg opened the menu.

"I obviously picked the wrong restaurant, but there wasn't a hot dog stand nearby. You're not going to find what you're looking for there," she said, taking his menu. "The food here is long on art and short on portions."

"Why don't you order for us."

"I could do that."

The hussar returned with their drinks. Caroline ordered a shrimp dish for Steeg and a Cobb salad for herself.

"I did some checking on you."

"And?"

"You're a violent man."

Steeg shrugged. "Everyone has to be good at something."

She passed him a large gray envelope.

"I'd like to hire you to look into my sister's murder."

"What's this?"

"Diana's picture. It will help catch her killer."

He opened the envelope and withdrew an eight-by-ten color photograph. The features were all there, but she just missed beautiful. Too sharp-edged. The mouth too tight. The eyes too mocking. He replaced the photo in the envelope and closed the clasp.

"I have a job," Steeg said.

"No, you don't."

"Got me again. Why me?"

"It's what you apparently do best."

"I do have other talents."

"I'm sure you do, but for now that's the only one that I find interesting."

"Fair enough. But if I decide to help, and that's a big if, it'll be because I want to, not because I'm being paid for it. But I'll need to know a lot more."

She nibbled on a breadstick.

"Okay, then, let's talk about Diana, Mr. Steeg."

"Steeg will do just fine."

"Where do I start?"

"What was she like?"

"Headstrong. The world wasn't big enough to contain her or her wants."

"A euphemism for —?"

"Daddy spoiled her. Gave in to her every whim."

Steeg sensed they were edging into "poor little rich girl" territory, a scenario that he found utterly boring, and one he had a difficult time relating to. Dominic had always worked two jobs, and still, there was never enough money.

"I didn't have that problem."

She continued as if she hadn't heard him. "After Mother's death, he changed. Everything changed."

"How so?"

"My father is a remote man, not given to outward displays of affection. The family curse. But with Mother's death, he showered Diana with attention as if she were the last of his line and his last chance at redemption."

"From the looks of the people who attended the memorial service, he's also a man with very powerful friends."

"Don't mistake a large checkbook with friendship."

"Where were you in all of this?"

"That's a very good question."

"Did you resent Diana?"

She set her breadstick aside.

"Why do I get the feeling I'm a suspect, Steeg?"

Actually, she was, along with her father and anyone else who entered Diana's orbit, but Steeg didn't tell her that.

"Old habits are hard to break."

"Actually, she and I were close. Perhaps I was looking for some residual attention from Daddy, a sort of 'halo of love' effect. At least that's what my shrink says. I had options, of course. I could have gone in many different directions, but I wound up as the good child, the long-suffering older sister. Anyway, I wasn't terribly surprised that her life ended like it did, in that man's apartment."

"How so."

Her voice softened. "When you lead the life Diana led, it's inevitable. Diana was adrift, a dust mote, a person to whom rules didn't apply. Her life was a litany of failure. In and out of schools, a few minor brushes with the police, a string of bad connections, men who used her and drugs that made them palatable."

The paunchy, oily image of Graham Moore flashed through Steeg's mind.

"Older men?"

"Progressively."

"Did you know Graham Moore?"

"The man himself? No. His incarnations? It was hard not to. She always had two or three going at once. There were so many late-night calls, pleas for help, promises made and broken. Her life was a cheap novel."

"Tell me about your mother."

"I barely remember her. I was eight when she . . . died. Diana was four. It changed everything."

"Your father never remarried?"
"No woman could possibly compete."
"With your mother?"
"With Diana."

CHAPTER ELEVEN

For someone with a lot of time on his hands, Steeg's plate was filling up rather nicely. He had a murder, a possible murder, and a missing Herkie to deal with. Linda and Diana Strickland weren't going anywhere anytime soon unless they were Raptured. Dead was indeed dead, Steeg reminded himself. So Herkie moved to the top of his To Do list. He was a pain-in-the-ass homeless guy, in a city filled with pain-in-the-ass homeless guys, but Steeg felt responsible for him. And the nature of his disappearance violated a deep Manichean streak in Steeg's ordered universe. Light versus dark. Right versus wrong. Weak versus strong. Bad guys coming out on top.

There was something else, though. Something Herkie had said. The bit of Rupert Brooke's poetry he had recited. Steeg didn't remember the words, but he didn't miss the sense. Herkie was trying to tell him something. The snatch of poetry was an elegy. An oration on death.

Normally, when people went missing, friends and associates would be interviewed, the neighborhood canvassed for witnesses, and hospitals checked for recent admissions. But there was nothing normal about Herkie. Friends were out, ditto family; he had none, that Steeg knew of. Under the best of circumstances Herkie was tough for anyone to take for extended periods of time. Sal had no idea where he had gone, and Dman was probably telling the truth. And that left Steeg exactly nowhere. Scouring the city wasn't an option; there was no telling where and if he'd find him. People like Herkie lived in the air, blown by the whims of the breeze, leaving no footprints. But one possibility remained, and Steeg grabbed it.

New York City's recycling laws required that garbage be separated into recyclables and ordinary trash; one more bullshit quality-of-life law in a city choking on quality-of-life laws. Recyclables included bottles and aluminum cans that could be exchanged at a nickel a pop. Stores didn't want them. Storing them was an open invitation for rats to attend a sugar party. Almost overnight, a new industry was born, staffed almost entirely by armies of enterprising homeless who spent their days picking through garbage. A slice of the Third World in Little Old New York. Crammed into huge black plastic lawn bags, the bottles and cans were lugged into recycling centers, exchanged for cash, and pounded into cubes by enormous compactors. A long run to a short slide. Five cents apiece translated to twenty cans and bottles. The math didn't favor the homeless.

C&C was the largest intake center on the West Side.

The place was noisy and smelled of hopelessness, a Diane Arbus photo panorama of Hell, and confirming yet again for Steeg the absence of a loving deity.

Steeg spotted a man wearing a dark green uniform and knee-high rubber boots, waving his arms and shouting orders. He walked up to him and asked for the manager. He was directed to a moldy office with a wraparound glass window in the back.

A burly man with a thick line of eyebrow extending across his forehead watched Steeg approach. He came out of the office and closed the door behind him.

"What?" the burly guy said, folding his arms across his chest.

Unpromising body language, Steeg thought.

"Need some information."

"Get lost."

Steeg sighed.

"Would it matter if I told you I was a cop?"

"It wouldn't matter if you told me you were the fuckin' Pope."

Kicking the living shit out of him, while appealing, would only result in short-term gratification and long-term grief. The cops would get involved, and Braddock would have another nail to hammer into the coffin that held what was left of his career. Steeg opted for short-term — it was more interesting.

"Yeah, but the Pope wouldn't throw you into the compactor." Steeg flashed an evil smile. "Best of all, it'll be our little secret."

The manager took a long moment measuring Steeg's size and the dead cast to his eyes. His arms unfolded and slowly dropped to his sides.

"Are you nuts?"

"Some have claimed."

He briefly considered his options. Fight, flight, or give the maniac what he wanted. It was an easy choice.

"I don't believe this shit. What do you wanna know?"

"How about we start with your name?"

"My name?"

He hesitated as if sensing that giving up this piece of vital information would open him up to a world of grief. But there was no way around it. "Frank," he finally said. "Frank Bonfiglio."

"Bonfiglio," Steeg repeated. "Means the good son, right? It's a strong name. Very euphonious. Okay, Frank, good to meet you. My name's Steeg. Now, Miguel and Santo. Have they been by today?"

"It wasn't my week to watch them. Do you think I keep a guest registry?"

Steeg had to admire the guy's balls.

"Are we being obstinate again?"

"Like I need this," Frank said. "I'll check. You wait here."

"You bet, Frank."

In a few minutes, Bonfiglio was back. "They're here."

Steeg smiled. "Now, wasn't that easy? Where?"

Bonfiglio pointed a finger at an oversized Dumpster filled with plastic water bottles.

The concept of bottled water was a continuing source of mystery for Steeg. Why people pay four times the price of a gallon of gas for perfectly refreshing, thirst-quenching water that came free from the tap eluded him.

"Over there. Now, can I get back to work?"

"Frank, the NYPD is grateful for your cooperation.

It's concerned citizens like you who make our jobs easier."

"You are fuckin' nuts," Bonfiglio said, retreating to the safety of his office.

Steeg found Miguel and Santo easily enough. Together, they bore a striking resemblance to Don Quixote and his trusty squire, Sancho Panza. Miguel was tall and cadaverous, while Santo was short and round.

Steeg walked up to them. "*Que pasa, amigos.*"

Their eyes narrowed. Miguel asked the question that was on everyone's mind lately. "What do you want?"

"I'm Herkie's friend and I'm looking for him. If you know where he is, I'd sure appreciate a heads-up."

"Herkie don't have friends."

"I know, but I'm the closest thing he has."

"Fuck off," Santo piped up.

This was definitely one of those days.

Steeg reached into his pocket and came out with some cash. He peeled off two tens and held them up.

"Any ideas?"

Miguel snatched them from his hand.

"He's got a new location. Down by the Port Authority. Says it's a better neighborhood. Safer."

Not by a long shot, Steeg knew.

The area around the Port Authority Bus Terminal was as bad as it gets in Hell's Kitchen. Anyone taking a bus into Manhattan ran a daily gauntlet of pimps trolling for runaways, profoundly crazy people baying at the moon, and the homeless encampment that circled the building like a shroud. Despite periodic attempts to clean the area up, the people who had no place else to go kept coming back.

Steeg found Herkie huddled under a green-painted plywood scaffold overhang. He had a new shopping cart.

"See you got new wheels," Steeg said.

"Very observant," Herkie replied, looking right past Steeg. "How'd you find me?"

"Miguel and Santo."

"Fucking Jacobins!"

"I'm sorry about what happened to you."

"Me too."

"Dman won't bother you again."

"Peachy."

"I have your books."

His gaze strayed to Steeg. "You do?"

"Well, not all of them. I mean, some of them were pretty beat up."

He rubbed a golf ball-sized lump over his right eye. "They weren't the only thing."

"But here's the thing. Dman recognized the error of his ways and agreed to replace every one."

Herkie's face softened, and his eyes widened with skeptical surprise. "He did?"

"Yep." Steeg patted his pocket. "I got the money right here."

He held out his hand. "Give it to me."

"Not a chance."

"You don't trust me?"

"No, you'd spend it on dope."

"Not all of it."

"Here's the deal. I figure we'll go shopping together, y'know, boys' night out. Okay?"

"Who can argue with the man with the money?"

"So, when are you moving back?"

"You sure about Dman, he won't fuck with me again?"

"You have my word."

"Why are you doing this?"

"You're like the son I never had."

Herkie did something Steeg had never seen him do. He smiled.

"Something's been bothering me. Remember that Rupert Brooke poem you recited for me?"

"Yeah. You want to hear it again?"

"Was it just something that popped into your mind, or were you being cryptic?"

Herkie got to his feet. "For a guy who thinks he's smart, you don't know shit, Steeg. Poetry isn't cryptic, it's the sound of the soul crying."

"Whose soul, Herkie?

Herkie looked away. "I saw them arguing."

"Who?"

"The girl and the guy who lives in your building."

"What were they arguing about?"

"What do pimps usually argue with their bitches about?"

CHAPTER TWELVE

"Why aren't you spendin' your leisure time frolickin' and gambolin' like a normal human being 'stead of gettin' involved in this stuff?"

Steeg and Luce sat in her unmarked in the middle of a whiteout. The heater was working overtime. Tiny flakes of snow were coming down so fast, the wipers couldn't keep up. The only other vehicles on the road were busses and cabs skidding their way along Eighth Avenue. The plows had yet to make an appearance.

"It's not normal, Steeg," she continued. "This should be a vacation for you, mon. 'Stead, you're sittin' with me wantin' to talk business."

Thumbing her nose at the weather, she wore a bright yellow suit and emerald green blouse under her heavy woolen overcoat. Large strawberry earrings completed the ensemble.

Steeg drained his Coke, crumpled up his napkin, and stuffed it in the ashtray. "You want another hot dog?"

"Three's my limit. A girl's got to watch her figure."

"Why is it hot dogs from a street cart taste better than when you make them at home?"

"The crap floating in the air flavors the water."

Steeg was still hungry but didn't feel like getting out of the car and into the storm. He could have asked the vendor to duck out from under the cart's umbrella and bring one over, but it seemed elitist. A dilemma.

"So, you got anything for me?"

"Yeah, a tip. Get some sun. Your skin's the color of worm flesh."

Steeg really wanted another hot dog.

"Be right back," he said, bolting from the car.

Luce turned the windshield wipers off; it was a losing battle, anyway.

The door swung open, and Steeg was back in his seat with two hot dogs wrapped in a napkin.

"I brought an extra in case you change you mind."

She reached over and snatched it from his hand. "Onions and mustard — a nice change of pace."

He took a small bite off the end. "Piquant and faintly amusing. Don't you think?"

Luce took a bigger bite. "A surprising blend of flavors."

"I did some sleuthing."

"Did you now?"

A smug smile wreathed his face. "Proud of me?"

Luce finished the rest of her hot dog and dabbed at the corners of her mouth with the napkin. "Is there a point here somewhere? Unlike you, I've got to get back to work."

"My C.I. tells me that young Miss Strickland was a hooker and my neighbor was her pimp. Seems she was working at Pinky's, that new lap-dance club on Twelfth."

"The one that's owned by what's-his-name, you know, the porn king?"

"Lenny Roberts, the very same. Apparently, he's cross-marketing his Pinky's magazine, CDs and videos, and sex toys with the club. The guy's a genius. Kind of like a Michael Eisner Disneyland operation for guys with hard-ons."

"That sounds awfully screwed up."

"There's more. The C.I. told me he saw them arguing the night of the murder. Seems she wanted to call it a night, and he didn't. That makes him, I believe, the last person to see her alive — and a suspect, if I remember Police Work 101 correctly."

"How does he know she was hookin'? Could be she was a girlfriend."

"My guy gets around, kind of blends in so you hardly notice him. Says he saw her in the alley back of the club with her johns."

"Doin' it against the wall?"

"Backseat of their cars. The money was passed to Moore, and he held the door open for her."

"Sounds like a gentleman."

"In my book."

"Well, I don't want to shock you, but I've done some sleuthin', too," Luce said.

"Really!"

"Yep. Not only was Mr. Moore a purveyor of young flesh, he was also a close associate of Councilman Terry Sloan and a regular at the Hudson Democratic Club."

"I notice that you're using the past tense."

"Mr. Moore was fished out of the water off the Battery early this mornin'. The Department has put a tight lid on it for now."

The news about Moore wasn't surprising, but his connection with the Hudson Democratic Club added a whole new wrinkle. The club was Terry Sloan's headquarters.

"That means it was possible he didn't murder the Strickland girl."

"Possible. Or he did, and made a really bad mistake and paid for it."

"Or it was a contract thing and he had to go."

"Or it was cock robin who did her in. Ain't police work fun?" She grew serious. "There's one other thing, Jackson, and I don't know exactly how to say it."

"That's never been a problem for you in the past."

"This is different. Braddock called me in. Gave me a new assignment."

Her relationship with Steeg had finally cost her, and he was deeply sorry.

"I didn't —"

"Let me finish. It's not what you think. You must be pissin' a lot of real important people off."

"That's been my M.O."

"My new assignment is you, and I've got a suspicion it wasn't his idea."

CHAPTER THIRTEEN

The Hudson Democratic Club had its roots firmly planted in the late nineteenth century during a time when Boss Tweed used the city as his personal ATM. In those days, the club was named the American Eagle Club, just like the coin. It was somehow fitting.

Tweed's monument to cost overruns was the Tweed Courthouse, on Chambers Street. Budgeted at $150,000, it tipped the scales at a whopping $13 million, quite a hunk of change when a nickel bought a schooner of beer and lunch. Most of the money found its way into his pockets. Eventually jailed for excessively sticky fingers, even by Tammany standards, Tweed had the last laugh. A little over a hundred years later, the three-and-a-half-story building was declared a landmark and now houses New York City's Department of Education, a civics lesson that keeps on giving.

You can't make this up, Steeg thought.

When the reformers finally kicked Tammany out, they moved their own Tweeds in, with bosses like Terry Sloan calling the shots. The "outs" became the "ins," and the "ins" became the "outs." It was enough to make your head hurt, and it was business as usual at the same old stand.

The club consisted of a large room with a couple of beat-up metal desks and several smaller offices around its periphery. Very unassuming and very politically correct. Never show the body public that the pols live better than they do.

Sloan's office, the only one with a door, was in the corner. The door was closed. The place was nearly empty, owing to the weather and the fact that it wasn't an election year. Four men in shirtsleeves and loosened ties sitting out no-show city jobs played pinochle at a desk.

Unlike them, Steeg had to play his cards close to the vest. The news of Moore's death probably wouldn't hit the news until later on in the evening. If Steeg let on that he knew, it could expose a leak that would quickly be walked back to Luce. And he wasn't about to let that happen.

He interrupted the game.

"I'm looking for Terry Sloan."

The players exchanged nervous looks.

One of them, a thin, gray-haired man, rose from the table and went to Sloan's office. He knocked, and the door opened a crack. Steeg saw him in whispered conversation with someone on the other side. In a few moments the door opened and another man, equally gray-haired, with cold blue eyes recessed in a face filled with sharp angles, emerged.

Steeg recognized him immediately. Albert Mallus, Sloan's bagman and all-around go-to guy. Mallus's job was to handle matters of unpleasantness.

He had met Mallus twice before. Once at a barbecue at Dave's house and once at the station house when he had intervened in the arrest of a West Side precinct captain's son who had hijacked a truckload of bras. Steeg recalled that charges were never filed.

Mallus threw the pinochle players a look and the game broke up, then he turned to Steeg and tried smiling a welcome, but his eyes refused to cooperate.

"I know you. Dave Steeg's brother, Jack." He held out his hand. "How ya doin'?"

If Sloan weren't going to come out to play, then Mallus would have to do.

Steeg took his hand. It was calloused, a workingman's hand. He wasn't surprised.

"Good."

Mallus took Steeg by the arm and led him to one of the offices. "A little privacy."

He took a seat behind the desk and motioned for Steeg to sit opposite him. Steeg remained standing.

"What can I do for you?"

"I'm looking for Terry Sloan."

"He's not here."

"Somehow I guessed that."

Mallus had a peculiar way of drumming his fingers on the desk. His fingertips barely touched the surface, making a faint whispering noise.

"What do you want him for?"

The air was stale, smelling of cigarettes and damp.

"A couple of questions about Graham Moore. Like what does he do for you and Terry. You know, his job."

Steeg watched him closely.

"What's your interest in him?"

"Let's just say I'm doing a favor for a friend."

Mallus shrugged. "A little bit of this and a little bit of that. You know, mainly volunteer work."

And there it was. A thinly veiled defensiveness, the tone a bit too smug and cocksure.

"Could you be a little more specific?"

"Not really."

"Let me take a shot. Does 'a little bit of this and that' include pimping?"

Rivulets of melting snow carved grimy trails on the windowpane.

Mallus stood up. "Well, it's been nice seeing you, Jack. Don't make yourself a stranger."

Steeg was tired of playing games with this guy whose occupation was playing games.

"Sit . . . the . . . fuck . . . down."

Mallus sat.

Steeg put his hands on the desk and leaned forward. He was teetering on the edge of the vortex again. The dark mist was swirling up.

"A woman was killed in my building. I've been asked by the family to look into it. I have every reason to believe that Moore did her. He works for you. It's not a coincidence, and that stokes my curiosity."

The angles on Mallus's face rearranged themselves into a sharp point.

"Because of your brother, I'm going to cut you some slack. Don't go getting involved in things that don't concern you. The cops are handling it, and if I remember correctly, you're not a cop anymore and you don't have a P.I.

license. Leave the investigation to your betters and butt the hell out, Jack, it's not your business."

"My '*betters*'?"

"You know what I mean."

"You know what your problem is, Albert?"

Mallus stared at him, hard.

"You're much too self-effacing."

"Leave it alone, Steeg."

"And miss out on all the fun?"

"Then welcome to the shit storm."

On the way out, Steeg noticed that the door to Sloan's office was open. He caught a fleeting glimpse of Sloan just beyond the jamb. Gideon El was standing next to him.

Steeg arrived home to find DeeDee, bundled up in her puffy coat and New York Giants knit cap, waiting out front.

"What are you doing out in this weather?"

"Beats staying inside."

"Everything all right at home?"

"Not really."

"What's that supposed to mean?"

"Papi's in jail," she said in a small voice.

Steeg felt the darkness settling in.

"Did he touch you?"

She shook her head.

"He got into a fight in a bar. Cut the guy."

"Now what?"

She shrugged in a way that suggested that when you

expect nothing from life and you get it, you're never disappointed.

Steeg put his hand on her shoulder.

"I guess there's only one thing to do."

"What's that?"

"Let's go home."

CHAPTER FOURTEEN

Next to scamming dough from the electorate, launching crusades is what politicians do best. It gets them in front of some bullshit hot-button issue and distracts the citizenry from what's really going on. Taking sex out of the city was the former mayor's crusade to prettify Midtown for tourists and developers. It was like taking the fizz out of seltzer. Almost overnight the city went flat. West Side porn shops and XXX theaters closed, only to reopen in less visible spots, like near the tunnels and other equally grubby locales. It just meant that the tourists and assorted locals had to work a little harder to find their pleasures.

Knowing it was just a matter of time until a new mayor showed up wielding the righteous sword of a new crusade, the industry went underground and waited. In a couple of years, smoking was out, screwing was back in, and Fun City was fun again.

Lenny Roberts led the charge.

Roberts was an interesting guy, sort of Mick Jagger to Hugh Heffner's John Lennon. A product of the New Orleans mob, he started out as a head banger on the docks and eventually moved into pimping, quickly working his way up to the top levels of flesh peddling in the South-east. Like most mob guys, Roberts was an entrepreneur, looking for opportunities that could spin off huge amounts of money with the least amount of effort. Unlike most mob guys, Roberts had a brain. Sex was his business, and he had a keen understanding of his customers' shifting tastes. The airbrushed white bread of Heffner and Guccione were over. The market was ready for the next new thing, and Pinky's was born, all chrome and Euro and surgically enhanced girl toys; a sex club for the twenty-first century.

After his failed campaign of shock and awe at the Hudson Democratic Club, Steeg didn't want to make the same mistake twice. All he had was Herkie's word that Diana was working at Pinky's and hooking for Moore, and that was hardly bankable. Very strange people hung out in Herkie's addled mind. Steeg needed confirmation about Diana, and the only place he was going to get it was Pinky's, and therein was the problem. He needed someone to talk to, someone in charge. That led him to Dave.

Although business was something they never discussed, Pinky's was more in Dave's world than his, and Dave knew lots of people. Steeg called him and asked for a name, no reasons given and no questions asked. Dave made a joking reference to Steeg's bull-in-a-china-shop performance at the Hudson Democratic Club and said he would get back to him. It took a day.

Pinky's looked to be about the size of a football field. There was an elevated stage in the center, with six goal-post-sized chrome poles on which writhed six topless beauties to a driving drumbeat of taped club music. Surrounding the stage were small tables and banquettes filled with the lunch hour crowd. The place smelled of testosterone. Working the rim of the stage was a pretty redhead with breasts the size of basketballs, contorting her body in ways Steeg didn't think possible. Red-faced men trying to cop a feel stuffed tens and twenties in her dental floss thong. Separate lap-dance rooms were set discreetly behind red velvet curtains off the main room.

Along the back wall and totally ignored was a buffet table with sad trays of canapés — swipes of tuna salad on toast points — allowing Pinky's to bill itself as a private gentlemen's eating club.

Steeg gave his name to the steroid freak with a shaved head and diamond stud in his left earlobe guarding the door. He passed Steeg on to a guy bearing a striking resemblance to a Bonobo monkey. Steeg followed him past the buffet table through a door that led backstage, taking him through the common dressing room filled with young women in various states of undress. They didn't give Steeg a look.

"I'd like to get my hands on some of that," Monkey Boy said.

"I'd say it's a long shot. Definitely."

"Why's that?"

"They probably go for guys with opposable thumbs."

Monkey Boy flashed him a blank stare.

At the far end of the dressing room was a closed door. Monkey Boy knocked, announced Steeg, opened the door, and left.

"Come on in," a gravelly voice boomed.

The office reminded Steeg of Graham Moore's apartment — it was in dire need of serious thought. There was a wooden desk filled with papers, a ratty green sofa that Steeg assumed had seen a fair number of auditions, and a Bed Bath & Beyond Oriental area rug. Sitting behind the desk was a human rectangle with short arms, stumpy legs, and a head the size of a volleyball. A star sapphire surrounded by tiny diamonds in a white gold setting gleamed on the ring finger of his right hand.

"Joey Rizzo. Take a seat."

Steeg looked around for a chair and, finding none, settled, not without misgivings, for the sofa. "Thanks for seeing me."

"They tell me that Dave's a good guy. That's why I'm seein' ya."

"Salt of the earth," Steeg agreed.

"What can I do for you?"

Steeg passed Diana Strickland's photo to him.

Rizzo barely glanced at it.

"You want a drink?"

"A Coke will be fine," Steeg said.

Rizzo put on an expansive smile.

"Hey, I'm buyin'. How about some single-malt?"

Steeg waved him off.

"A Coke will do the trick."

"Whatever." Rizzo picked up the phone. "Get me my usual and a Coke for my friend."

It's good to make new friends, Steeg thought.

"Could you take a look at the photo and tell me if you know her?"

Rizzo picked up the photograph. His mouth tightened, and his eyes narrowed in concentration. It was like watching a neurologist studying a CAT scan. Rizzo was trying too hard.

There was a knock on the door, and a second or two later it opened. It was the redhead contortionist carrying their drinks on a small, round tray that could easily have been balanced on her breasts. She walked in, did a pretty fair imitation of a bunny dip, and set the tray on Rizzo's desk. This time she was fully dressed. In addition to the thong, she wore a skimpy bra.

Rizzo put the photo down.

"Anything else?" she said.

Rizzo dismissed her with a shake of his head. When the door closed behind her, he picked up the photo and handed it to Steeg. "Never saw her before. Pretty, though."

"That's too bad, I was hoping you could help."

"Is she anything to you?"

"A friend of a friend."

Rizzo stood up, signaling the end of the meeting.

"I got things to do, you know. But you can hang around outside. If you're a friend of Dave's, consider yourself comped."

Steeg got up, too. He took the photo, turned it face-down, pulled a pen out of his pocket, and wrote "Jackson" and his phone number. Rizzo didn't make the filial connection and there was no reason to tip him off.

"I got plenty more of these. Why don't you pass it around and see if anyone knows her. My name and number are on the back."

"Sure," Rizzo said. "I'll ask the girls. You never know, right?"

Steeg knew that as soon as he left, the photo was headed straight for the trash.

"You never know," Steeg agreed.

"So I guess you got what you came for and I won't be seeing you again."

"Don't bet on it, but for now I guess I've got to look for other Dumpsters to dive in."

Steeg's comment brought Rizzo up short.

"You got a problem with my business?"

"You might say."

Rizzo's dark eyes glinted.

"Number one, it ain't none of your business. Number two, I give the customers what they want. No harm, no foul, and no victims."

Steeg had heard that story before. Before joining Homicide he had worked Vice very briefly and had transferred to Homicide when he couldn't take it anymore. That Homicide, outright murder, was a step up the food chain was mind-boggling. In many ways, prostitution was just as heinous. The trouble with "the oldest profession" — a term that euphemized degradation — was that it robbed its practitioners of their voice, their power, and their humanity. Men like Rizzo turned his stomach.

"The first thing I'm going to do when I leave here is take a shower."

Rizzo remained silent, but Steeg could see that it was difficult.

On the way out of Pinky's, the redhead sidled up to him.

"I saw the picture on Joey's desk," she whispered.

"She was my friend. Now give me a big smile and pretend that you like me."

"I do like you. But tell me about the girl in the picture."

She appeared frightened.

"Not here."

She led him through the curtains into a lap-dance room and sat him in an upholstered chair.

"What kind of music do you like?"

"Something really dreary. Got 'Sunday Morning Coming Down,' by Willie Nelson?"

"Fresh out."

She hit a button on a console and turned the volume of something erotically cheery way up, then walked over to Steeg and straddled him.

A grotesque, but enlightening, way to conduct an interview.

CHAPTER FIFTEEN

Venus—not a bad choice of names for someone in her line of work—was terrified, and she had every reason to be. Rizzo was a hard man with a mean streak. From what Steeg was able to piece together, contrary to the story floating around, Lenny Roberts never gave up his network of brothels. It had expanded and was a kind of a minor-league, feeding fresh talent into Pinky's, which was very definitely the majors. Typical of so many of Roberts's girls, Venus was a runaway from a small Alabama town — Litter Barrel, she mockingly called it — and was quickly recruited by one of Roberts's pimps. Pretty soon she was in the system. Chattanooga, Charlotte, Dallas, Atlanta, Chicago, Los Angeles, and finally graduation to Pinky's. The rules were simple—no drugs, legs open, mouth shut—and the penalties severe. Some girls were demoted to working interstate truck stops, others were sent out of the country, and some simply disappeared. According to Venus, Diana wasn't using drugs and did what she was told. Further, Moore wasn't exactly her pimp. Each of the girls was assigned to someone like Moore who made sure they stayed with the program. Now, Venus was worried that her friendship with Diana would put her on the same road, and she wanted out. Steeg gave her Luce's number and assured her she would help.

A couple of things didn't add up, though. How did Diana wind up working for Roberts? If she was as compliant as Venus claimed, why was she killed? And why did Moore have to go, too? What was the connection between Moore and Roberts and Terry Sloan? Finally, where did Gideon El fit in all this? Right now, they were open questions, but at least Steeg had enough information to get some of the answers from Caroline.

He called her, and they agreed to meet on his turf, Renzi, a quiet little restaurant with paper napkins on Tenth and Forty-first.

The snow had stopped, and the streets were rapidly turning into solder-gray goo.

"Very charming place. Smudged glasses, daily specials on a chalkboard. Lots of character, Steeg," Caroline said, examining her flatware for signs of plague.

"Renzi is a moveable feast."

She wore jeans tucked into high boots and an oversized, black ribbed sweater accentuating the creamy paleness of her skin. A thin gold chain circled her neck.

"Now, what was so important that I had to schlep all the way over here?"

Steeg couldn't decide if her use of the Yiddish vernacular was an attempt to show that she was just one of the guys, or an act of condescension.

"You haven't been entirely honest with me," Steeg said.

She dipped a corner of her napkin into her glass of Peroni and vigorously rubbed her fork.

"How so?"

"You didn't tell me that Diana was a working girl."

She examined the fork closely and set it back on the table, then took in a draft of air and let it out slowly.

"Had it finally come to that?"

"Let's cut the bullshit. You know it had."

She lifted the glass of beer to her lips and drained it.

"I give you my word, I had no idea. I hadn't seen Diana in months. I assumed she was avoiding me. Now I know why. How did you find out?"

The waiter approached, and Steeg waved him off.

"Tell me about Diana. Tell me how somebody like her, coming from a family like yours, winds up selling her body."

"I'll need another beer."

Steeg motioned to the waiter for a refill.

"I've already told you that after our mother's death she changed from a vivacious, happy child to a rebellious little bitch. At first there were little things like tantrums and a fear of being left alone. Eventually, she graduated to setting fires, shoplifting, unexplained absences. You name it, she did it, and Daddy put up with it. We both put up with it. Diana and I were once so close, but then she began to drift away."

Steeg remained silent.

"It was only when her behavior became self-destructive that we finally did something about it."

"Self-destructive, how?"

95

"She was twelve and attending the Porter School. Apparently, she hooked up with a group of kids who fashioned themselves Goths, or some such thing. You know how kids at these schools are."

"No, I don't. We were blessed with poverty."

She allowed herself a small smile.

"In place of quality time, the kids are showered with Mommy and Daddy's money, allowing them to indulge their often outlandish fantasies. Like water seeking its own level, the kids divide up into groups. You have your preppies, nerds, and scholarship students who no one bothers with, dopers, gangsters, and Goths."

"No Vandals, Huns, Celts, or Franks?"

"These kids are rich, not creative. Anyway, Goths are into black clothes, face painting, weird music, and self-mutilation. You know, like body piercing. They look like refugees from *The Addams Family*."

"Seems stupid but harmless."

"Not when the ante is raised to suicide."

"Diana tried to kill herself?"

"Several times over the years."

"I'm no expert on these things, but when you put it all together it seems like there was a lot of self-loathing there. How did your father handle it?"

"Not well. At first he was in complete denial. 'Typical adolescent behavior,' he called it."

"Suicide?"

"You've got to know my father. Eventually, he packed her off to a psychiatrist."

"Name?"

"Sheila Weldon. Has an office on Fifth, but she'll never talk to you."

"Yes, she will," Steeg said.

"I tried, Steeg. I really did, but Diana was closed in. Kept everything inside. It was as if she had constructed a world with bricks of rage and eventually it consumed her. When she was eighteen she moved out and went her own way. Money wasn't an issue — there was enough in her trust fund to last three lifetimes." Her eyes filled with tears. "It's so damned sad!"

In that moment something showed through. The WASP ice queen façade had crumbled, revealing, for the first time, a sister's grief.

He passed her his napkin. "How did she get along with your father?"

She dabbed at her eyes. "She despised him."

"Why?"

"I don't know. She wouldn't say."

"And you, how do you feel about him?"

"Where's this going, Steeg?"

"I don't know. I figure the more questions I ask, the better the odds of finding out something that leads somewhere. It's just how the process works."

"Diana was his favorite; I was an afterthought."

Steeg let that comment go, but planned to revisit it another time. Besides, there was another area he wanted to explore.

"Tell me about your mother."

"Not much to tell. I barely remember her. The only memories I have are stored in old photographs."

"How did your parents meet?"

"How do children of the rich usually meet? Coming out parties? School? The whole point is to merge the family fortunes and, at the very least, keep them intact. There's lots of inbreeding going on."

"I know what you mean. Have you seen pictures of the House of Windsor lately? One more generation and their chins are completely gone." He paused. "One more question."

She waved a hand as if she were swatting flies. "No more questions. You're wearing me out."

Steeg put his hands up, palms out.

"You're right, enough for one day. How about something to eat? Everything is good, but if you like garlic, the chicken scarpariello is incomparable."

"I'm not hungry."

"Okay. What would you like to do?"

Her eyes hinted a smile.

"You."

It was a tough offer to refuse.

Herkie was as nervous and goggle-eyed as a kid on his first trip to the candy store. Steeg had left Caroline's apartment in such a good mood that he wanted to spread some sunshine. Recalling his promise to Herkie, it seemed like a plan, and he went looking for him. On his way to the Port Authority Bus Terminal, he called his home answering machine for messages. There was one from Luce. The M.E.'s report was in on Diana, and Luce didn't want to talk about it on the phone. He called her back and told her to meet him at the Gotham Bookstore at

4:00, figuring it would give him enough time to find Herkie and neaten him up a bit.

Steeg found him sitting in the same spot under the plywood overhang. His cart was gone — probably was swiped while he was sleeping. He took him back to his apartment, got him showered and shaved, and got some food into him. A quick stop at possibly the last army-navy store in the city made Herkie more than presentable. For a few hundred dollars Steeg decked him out in a heavy winter coat, jeans, turtleneck sweater, woolen navy watch cap, plaid shirt, wool-lined leather gloves, and thick-soled boots. It was the first set of new clothes Herkie had worn in years. He even smelled good.

At 4:00 they were inside the store, waiting for Luce.

"I'm really nervous," Herkie said. He didn't know quite what to do with his hands. They went in and out of his pockets like he had misplaced something and didn't remember where he had put it.

"It'll pass."

"I don't remember the last time I've been in a place like this."

"Yeah, well, it's your day."

"Can I really buy them new?"

"Sure."

Herkie closed his mouth and took a deep swig of air in through his nose.

"You know what it smells like in here, Steeg?"

It smelled stale and musty, but Steeg wasn't about to be accused of being a mood breaker again. "Smells good."

"No," Herkie said, his eyes going dreamy. "Life, Steeg. It smells of life. When you open a new book for the first time and you hear the spine crack, it's like a birth pang. And then you bring it so close to your face that your nose is buried in it and you smell life."

Steeg gave Herkie's back an affectionate rub.

"Why don't you check the place out while I wait for Luce. Okay?"

"She's a cop, huh?"

"My partner."

Herkie nodded. "One of the good guys, right? Not going to hurt me."

"She's not going to hurt you."

So caught up in the wonder of it all, Herkie missed the crack in Steeg's voice that had grown suddenly small.

Steeg walked outside to compose himself. A few minutes later, Luce pulled up in front of the Gotham, parking next to a hydrant partially buried under a mound of soot-streaked snow. She pulled the NYPD placard off the visor, set it on the dashboard, and got out of her unmarked.

"What was the M.E.'s verdict?"

"You sure don't waste time on pleasantries. Overdose."

"Venus said she didn't do drugs."

Luce was mystified. "Who's Venus?"

He didn't figure she would call Luce — they rarely do. Once in, it's hard to get out, like kicking a jones.

"Nobody."

"Apparently it was a hot shot. She had enough heroin in her to feed the junkies in Bed-Stuy for a week. Injected her in a vein near her groin. Hard to spot."

"So, she didn't do it herself."

"Uh-uh. Arms clean as a baby's ass. Sniffin' cocaine her deal. Nasal membranes all shot to hell, bridge of her nose near collapse. Someone did her. Ain't no woman gonna shoot shit in her snatch 'less she wore out all of her veins."

"And Moore?"

"Nothin' new, 'cept it was a professional job. Done him with a couple of .22s. They go in and bounce around inside the skull until they turn the brain to grits, but you know that. That's it. Abbot and Costello are on the case. Come the next millennium they'll have somethin'."

Steeg shrugged. "Come inside, I want you to meet Herkie."

"The crazy guy?"

"One and the same."

Steeg led her into the bookstore and found Herkie in the poetry section. The basket at his feet was four deep with books.

Not wanting to startle him, from a few feet away, Steeg called his name.

"Herkie!"

He closed the book he was reading and turned around.

"There's someone I want you to meet."

Herkie held the book out to Steeg. "Did you ever read Gerard Manley Hopkins? He's a Catholic like you."

As Steeg recalled, Hopkins was very big at Precious Blood. Required reading.

"Yeah, lots of alliteration. You know, 'dappled, dimpled, dawn' — not my taste."

Herkie withered him with a look.

"Asshole! What the hell do you know?" He placed the book carefully into the basket.

"Charming fellow," Luce whispered.

"Some people have often mistaken him for Dale Carnegie."

"Herkie, I want you to meet my partner, Luce Guidry. Luce, this is Herkie."

She put on her brightest smile.

"Hello, Herkie."

Herkie checked her out, his gaze roving from Luce's stem to her stern. "You wanna fuck?"

Steeg had to hand it to her — she kept her smile in place and didn't even as much as flinch.

"I don't think so, but thanks for asking."

"Why not?"

"You're not my type."

That seemed to satisfy him, almost.

"You got a sister?"

Luce's smile grew even broader.

"'Fraid not. I'm an only child."

"Me too. I made you angry, though."

"No, you didn't."

"I do that sometimes. Make people angry, and then they do bad things."

"What bad things?"

"They hurt me."

CHAPTER SIXTEEN

Thinking that at least one person in his newly expanded household ought to have an ordered life, Steeg gave DeeDee the bedroom and a new TV, moved to the living room sofa, and divvied up housekeeping responsibilities. She was responsible for her homework, making up her bed, and picking up after herself. He handled everything else. That took care of the day-to-day. The more pressing issue was their relationship. Children's Protective Services notwithstanding — a bridge he would have to cross sooner or later — she was now his responsibility, but he had no idea what that meant. She wasn't his roommate, and he wasn't her father; the answer was somewhere in between, and they would just have to figure it out. Besides, he reminded himself, it was a temporary arrangement.

It had started off well, as good-intentioned plans often do, but once the novelty wore off, DeeDee and Steeg reverted to form. The erstwhile DeeDee turned into a teenager, and Steeg turned into his mother.

Conversations took on a monosyllabic quality, her clothes had migrated all over the apartment, MTV was on the tube, and rap music blasted from her room. It was getting so bad, he was beginning to learn the words.

On a frigid Sunday afternoon, Steeg took matters into his own hands. He knocked on her bedroom door, strode in, and snapped off the TV.

From her spot on the bed, propped up on pillows and surrounded by a menagerie of stuffed animals, she regarded him with suspicion.

"What'd you do that for?"

"We have to talk."

She reached for the remote and clicked the TV on. A guy Steeg was sure he had sent to Rikers a few years ago for armed robbery rapped about bitches and hos.

"Sure," she said, in a tone suggesting that a talk was the last thing on her schedule.

He pulled the plug out of the wall.

"Why do you like this crap?"

She let out a "here we go" sigh. "It's my music."

Wrong approach! Steeg had a sudden flashback to his teens. When the same question was posed by his parents, his response had been exactly the same.

"What do you like to do?"

"What I'm doing," she said, setting the trap.

"Your brain is rotting."

She raised a dismissive eyebrow, and the trap snapped shut. "Weren't you just watching the Giants game? Talk about brain rot! I mean, they really suck."

She had him, and he was running out of approaches.

"How about hobbies?"

More raised eyebrows.

"How about plugging the set back in?"

"That's it. Put your coat on, we're going out."

Nolan's Gym, on Ninth Avenue and Forty-first, occupied the second floor of a Hasidic-run discount electronics store.

The sun was low in the sky and so bright, it hurt the eyes.

"What are we doing here?" she asked.

"It's important."

They walked up a flight of stairs and opened the metal door leading into the gym. Immediately, they were enveloped in a wave of heat. The air had the rank smell of sweat and the sharpness of liniment.

Nolan's was a throwback to the time when boxing was a big deal in New York, with fight clubs all over the city, and bouts just about every night of the week. But times had changed. HBO and Showtime ran boxing now, and big-payday fights were few and far between. The walls were papered in yellowing posters, and the ceiling was in need of repair. Two short, sinewy Hispanic fighters were whacking the hell out of each other in a large ring set in the middle of the wooden floor. Off to the side, other fighters were stretching, slamming the heavy bags or blowing their noses into their fingers.

"Welcome to Nolan's."

DeeDee sniffed the air and made a face.

"It smells like something died."

Steeg had to agree. "You'll get used to it."

Her eyes narrowed. "What does that mean?"

"Come on," he said, half-dragging her to the ring.

The bell sounded, and it was apparent the fighters needed a blow. One draped his arms on the ropes while the other bent over at the waist, trying to catch his breath. Their bodies glistened with sweat. Standing ringside with a stopwatch clenched in his fist, a short, stocky man in his seventies threw his hands up in disgust. The heavy scar tissue on his brow ridge and the thickness of his jaw gave his face a vaguely Neanderthal appearance.

"Oh, *laaadies*!" he yelled, in mocking singsong. "I asked for three good minutes and you give me a fuckin' ballet. Why the fuck I waste my time on you jokers is somethin' I can't figure out. I should just call Immigration and end the fuckin' misery."

"By my count, they gave you better'n six minutes," Steeg said. "Longest three minutes since Tunney beat Dempsey."

Nolan swung around.

"Mind your own . . . Steeg!" he smiled broadly, and then threw his arms around him in a sweaty hug. "How're you doin'? Long time no see."

"Good, Al. I see you're up to the same old tricks. Heat's about ninety-five, no headgear, long rounds. Nothing ever changes."

"Hey, it's a tough business." He waved his arm. "All these guys want is a payday, but they don't want to work for it."

"I want you to meet someone. DeeDee, this is Al Nolan. He runs the place and is the only Jew in New York with an Irish name. When he fought, the crowd wanted Irishmen, so he was Irish."

"He would have a lot tougher time if they wanted blacks," she said.

"She's got a mouth on her, that one," Nolan said, not without admiration.

"That's one of the reasons we're here."

"You want me to put her in with Rafael the Human Marshmallow over there," he said, gesturing to the fighter disentangling his body from the ropes.

DeeDee shrank back behind Steeg.

Steeg laughed. "It may have to come to that. I hear that you're branching out from boxing, you know, getting into the martial arts."

"Branching out, my ass. Oops! Excuse me, little girl. Can't make the rent anymore. Leasing some of the space to these karate and judo jokers. Whatever it takes, right? These morons I got in my stable can barely pass the State physical, and they want to fight. Give 'em a knife and they might have a chance. But with their fists? Uh-uh. Not like you used to be."

"That was a long time ago. I was young and stupid then."

"Yeah, but you could fight. Knew how to turn a punch."

DeeDee's eyes widened in astonishment. "You fought?"

"A little."

"Listen to Mr. Modesty over here. He was a Golden Gloves champ. Won it at the Garden. Next stop was the Nationals and then the Olympics. Steeg was a natural."

"Yeah," he said, mimicking the Marlon Brando role in *On the Waterfront*. "I coulda been a contender, but all I got was a one-way ticket to Palookaville."

"Don't listen to him, little girl. He was a good one. A thinker in there. No one ever got more out of a punch than him."

This is getting embarrassing, Steeg thought. "It's been a great trip down memory lane, but I need a favor, Al."

"Just name it."

"Do you have a guy who teaches tae kwon do?"

"Yeah, I think the karate guy does that, too. Why, are you getting into that Oriental shit?"

"It's not for me, it's for DeeDee."

She took a few steps back. "Me?"

"Yeah, it's good exercise for your body and your mind."

"I don't think so," she said.

"I do. And if that doesn't work, we'll move on to scrapbooking or stamps, but we're going to find something that you're interested in or die trying."

"Don't I have a say in this?"

"No. You live with me, you follow the house rules." He turned to Nolan. "Could you set it up?"

"Sure, I'll call you tomorrow. You're still in the book, right?"

"Unfortunately, yes."

On the way home, they stopped for Chinese takeout. DeeDee still wasn't convinced.

Steeg didn't care.

They climbed the stairs to Steeg's apartment. It was very quiet. Too quiet. When they reached his landing, Steeg saw him. He motioned for DeeDee to stay where she was.

Herkie was propped against the wall. A neat hole marked the center of his forehead. A thin stream of blood had managed to avoid the bridge of his nose and work its way under his left eye, as if it were the track of a tear.

His expression betrayed no hint of surprise.

CHAPTER SEVENTEEN

When Steeg and Ginny were still an item, they would pack a picnic hamper and subway it up to the Bronx for Woodlawn Cemetery's annual Fourth of July concert. What made it special was that only works by composers buried there were performed. Every summer Ellington, Cohan, W.C. "Daddy" Handy, Berlin, and Miles Davis got to jam together in an encore performance. Afterward, he and Ginny would place flowers on their graves.

Now Steeg was back, with DeeDee. Bunched-up clouds rode low in the sky, and tiny whirlpools of dead leaves clattered like dry bones across the frozen ground.

There would be no unmarked grave on Hart Island for John Heinz Herkimer, Ph.D., Columbia University, of Fort Madison, Iowa. His grave was midway between Herman Melville's and Bat Masterson's.

Good company. Should make for some lively conversation.

After Herkie's death, Steeg had done some checking, and cursed himself for not doing it sooner. The Department of Defense had his records. Captain John Herkimer was awarded the Silver Star during Desert Storm. It explained his love of the War Poets. He was married briefly, but madness and drugs had put an end to it and landed him on the streets. Steeg tracked down his ex-wife, but Herkie was just a bad memory to her. He had no other family.

Steeg handled all of the arrangements, and Woodlawn supplied a nondenominational minister. There was no mention of God. The Great Trickster had a puckish sense of humor. He had given Herkie a first-class mind and then slipped in a bad gene to blow it all to hell. The Lord giveth and the Lord taketh. Blessed be the name of the Lord!

The good reverend's sermon was Siegfried Sassoon's poem, "How To Die," delivered while two gravediggers sat on a mound of dirt having a smoke.

Dark clouds are smouldering into red
   While down the craters morning burns.
The dying soldier shifts his head
   To watch the glory that returns;
He lifts his fingers toward the skies
   Where holy brightness breaks in flame;
Radiance reflected in his eyes,
   And on his lips a whispered name.

You'd think, to hear some people talk,
   That lads go West with sobs and curses,
And sullen faces white as chalk,
   Hankering for wreaths and tombs and hearses.
But they've been taught the way to do it

Like Christian soldiers; not with haste
And shuddering groans; but passing through it
With due regard for decent taste.

Crammed into the coffin was three hundred and seventy-five dollars' worth of books.

The minister, at a loss for something else to do, nodded his good-byes. The gravediggers pulled themselves to their feet and dug their shovels into the mound of dirt. DeeDee threw a rose onto the coffin. The petals scattered like droplets of blood.

It was time to leave.

"It isn't right," DeeDee said.

Steeg was reminded of a line famously attributed to Sam Goldwyn: "Pictures are for entertainment, messages should be delivered by Western Union." Herkie's death was a message that left Steeg with a knot in his heart and a fire in his brain. The people who did this would pay.

"I know."

"I mean, why Herkie? He never hurt no one."

"It wasn't about Herkie."

"What's that supposed to mean?"

"Whoever did this made a mistake. In a way, it's like boxing. When you get into the ring you don't fight the cornermen. You look to take the fighter out."

"I don't understand."

"I know."

CHAPTER EIGHTEEN

It was always there, a cold radiance, shimmering in the dark place where the snakes slept. Without warning, it blazed with the heat of a thousand suns, turning his brain to razor wire and his mouth to sand. The want had become need.

The snakes had come out to play. Finding an AA meeting or seeing his sponsor never crossed his mind. The only thing Steeg wanted to see was the bottom of a whiskey glass.

He found a bar.

It was very chi-chi, with chrome and black leather and parquet floors; a bar that served drinks with silly names that took too long to do the job. It was also a place where he wasn't known.

The thick-necked young bartender had moussed blond hair fashionably long on top and cut close on the sides.

Steeg slid onto a stool and set his palms flat on the ebony bar.

"Jack Black, neat." Just saying the words and hearing them delivered with certitude brought a small measure of relief.

The bartender nodded and slipped a napkin between Steeg's hands. Turning to the mirrored display behind him, he took his time finding and pulling a bottle off the glass shelf.

The tip of Steeg's tongue hungrily swept across his lips. They felt like sandpaper.

The bartender set a glass on the napkin. "Neat, you said." The voice betrayed Midwest roots.

Steeg nodded.

"I hear we're in for more snow," he said, finally pouring.

"Sure," Steeg managed to say, entranced by the familiar choreography of a saloon–the bottle tipped with a metal spout, the measured pour, the liquid gold swirling into the glass.

From force of habit he reached into his jacket pocket for a cigarette and, to his great surprise, found a fresh pack of Marlboros and a pack of matches. He had no memory of purchasing it and didn't dwell on it. He stripped the cellophane off, flipped the top open, pulled one out, and lit it. The smoke made him light-headed but felt good going down. It had been a very long time.

"Sorry, uh-uh. Can't do that here. Take it outside," the bartender said.

Steeg ignored him and reached for the glass. He tipped it back against his lips and drank hungrily. The liquid ignited the back of his throat, and in a few moments filled him with a seeping calm as it entered his bloodstream. It was a beginning and an end.

Closing his eyes, he took another pull on the cigarette. The nicotine spaciness was gone, replaced by an eerie sense of contentment. When he opened his eyes they were empty, a fact not lost on the bartender. Smiling without humor, he pulled out a twenty and laid it on the bar.

"Let it be our little secret." He tapped the glass, signaling a refill.

The bartender measured Steeg. Throwing his ass into the street didn't seem like a viable option. The guy was too tightly wound, a heat-seeking missile looking for a target of opportunity. He pocketed the bill.

"Okay, but you're gonna have to take it in the back. There's another room we use for parties and shit."

Steeg rose from the stool and pocketed his cigarettes. He tapped the glass on the bar. Hard.

"Fill her up."

The bartender obliged.

This time, Steeg drank more slowly, rolling it around in his mouth, savoring the smoky taste, feeling the darkness settle in.

He laid another twenty on the counter. "Give me the bottle and show me the room."

The church has high, vaulted ceilings. Steeg stands at the foot of the altar, alone. A faraway sound of chanting breaks the silence. A door opens. A cowled monk swinging a censer appears in the doorway. He pauses, then proceeds down the center aisle. Other monks, struggling under the weight of a large wooden crucifix bearing the body of Christ, enter. Blood streams from the thorns embedded in His forehead. The air is thick with smoke and the smell of incense.

Steeg's throat tightens with panic.

The chant grows louder as the procession nears the altar.

"One, two, three, four. We ain't gonna take no more!"

The leader reaches the altar and halts. The procession kneels. The crucifix slowly levitates, righting itself above them. The volume of the chant increases, filling the church.

"One, two, three, four. We ain't gonna take no more!"

Blood streams from a hole in the center of His forehead. Christ's face morphs into Herkie's.

Steeg tries to run, but a hand grips his shoulder. He fights to shrug it off, but the nails dig in. He glances back and sees a black fog creeping in, filling the church, and swallowing everything. But the hand grips tighter, the nails deeper, pulling him into the darkness, into the place where the snakes are waiting.

"Jackson, wake up! *Jackson!*"

Steeg forced his eyes open.

"There you go, Jackson, you're comin' back to us."

A dark face swam across his field of vision. His eyes squint into narrow slits to bring it into focus.

He tried to speak, but his mouth was gummy and foul tasting.

"Had us worried there," Luce said. "How're you feelin'?"

"Like . . . someone set my head on a kicking tee and

took field-goal practice," he croaked. "Where am I? What happened?"

"Still got a sense of humor. 'Bout the only thing you haven't puked up. You're home. 'Pears you threw yourself a little party and didn't bother to invite anyone."

A wave of nausea ripped through his guts.

Luce jumped back.

"Uh-uh," she said. "This outfit cost a lot of money. You gotta heave, use the pail right by your head."

He massaged his temples with the pads of his fingers, trying to erase the throbbing pain. "I did a bad thing."

"In a manner of speakin'."

"I remember coming home from the funeral and telling DeeDee that I needed to go out for a while. *DeeDee?* What the hell have I done?" He managed to prop himself up on an elbow, but the effort brought on a wave of dizziness and another spasm of nausea. "Where . . . is she?"

He followed Luce's gaze to a corner of the living room, where DeeDee sat on the hardwood floor with her arms wrapped tightly around her knees. Her face was hard with disappointment.

He tried to rise and go to her, but gave it up as a lost cause. "DeeDee, I didn't mean —"

She jumped to her feet and ran into her room, slamming the door behind her.

"You fucked up, Jackson. You really fucked up this time. It ain't all about you anymore. You're all this child has in the whole world. How's it gonna look when Children's Protective Services comes by to see how she's gettin' along. Whether you have a proper home for her. Whether you're fit to be takin' care of her. They ain't called yet 'cause they're more fucked up than you, but they will, and then what're you gonna do? You should be ashamed of yourself."

He was, and he'd have to find a way to make it right. "I know, I know. How'd you find me?"

"Don't know where you started out, but you ended up at the Liffey."

Steeg didn't remember where he'd started, either, but the Liffey was a cops' bar in Midtown. Old habits were hard to break, even when you're completely in the bag.

"Jimmy Finn called when he saw you come reelin' in, lookin' all deep and dark and smellin' like a latrine. Seems you took exception to his not wantin' to serve you."

"Did I do anything really stupid?"

"Jimmy said everything you did was really stupid."

"Perfect! Another friend down the drain. I'll drop by later and apologize."

"Not a good idea."

"Why not?"

"I'm not sure he wants to see you just yet. Let's just say you didn't exactly cover yourself with glory. By the way, Braddock's rat Petrovitch was there. Jackson, my friend, you know I love you to death. But, if you didn't have bad luck, you'd have no luck at all."

"That's it, then, I've really screwed the pooch this

time. The bastard is probably convening a Departmental trial as we speak. Well, it was fun while it lasted."

"Not quite. Told him if he opens his yap, I might have to send an anonymous letter to Internal Affairs about some of the scams he's got going."

"What kind of scams?"

"Beats me, but the stupid son of a bitch bought it."

"I owe you, Luce."

"Big-time."

Steeg managed to swing his feet to the floor.

"Where you goin'?" Luce asked.

"One, two, three, four. We ain't gonna take no more!"

"To the bathroom." He stopped. "What in hell is all that noise?"

"Your basic New York City demonstration."

"Here?"

Steeg staggered over to the window. The sky looked like the bottom of a garbage can.

Looking down, he saw that the front of his apartment house had been turned into a memorial for Herkie. Mounds of flowers lay on the stoop, and Gideon El, surrounded by about twenty followers, was holding forth. Steeg was in no mood for this. It felt as if someone were pounding roofing nails into his skull. He walked unsteadily to the bathroom and freshened up as best he could. One glance at the mirror told him he still had a long way to go. Without bothering to change his clothes, he headed toward the door.

"Where're you goin'?"

"To your basic New York City demonstration."

"You look like a bag lady," she said with disgust. "Let me get my coat and I'll go with you."

"Nope," he said. "I'm the one who needs some fresh air."

Before he left, he knocked on DeeDee's door. "DeeDee, are you all right?" he said.

No answer, but he didn't expect one.

"I'm going out for a few minutes, but I'd like to talk when I get back."

Same response.

He looked over at Luce for support.

She shrugged. "What do you expect when you act the fool?"

"Thanks for piling on. How much time do I have to do in the penalty box?"

"That's up to you, mon."

Steeg headed out the door.

Crews from all the local TV and radio stations were in attendance. Gideon El had turned them out as if he were a pop star.

"The mayor lives in his fancy townhouse with a fancy East Side address and treats Hell's Kitchen like it was some damned trailer park!" He said into the forest of outstretched microphones.

Nice line, Steeg thought.

"Well," Gideon El continued. "That's gonna stop, now."

As if on cue, the mob turned up the volume of the chant. *"One, two, three, four. We ain't gonna take no more!"*

Steeg, did a quick scan of the crowd. The only familiar face belonged to Dman lingering back on the fringe. Onlooker? Maybe, Steeg thought. Or maybe not.

"We've had three killings in the past two weeks. All homeless folks. Who's next?"

This was a new wrinkle. Three homeless people. If he was right, it could be a serial killer, or a gang of kids looking for a little excitement. He'd have to check with Luce to see if the NYPD was on it.

"I want the mayor to hear this loud and clear." His voice elevated a couple of octaves. "If he won't protect us, then we're gonna have to do it ourselves."

The chant picked up again, louder and angrier, until the demonstrators finally ran out of steam.

The show was over.

Reporters had their sound bites, their crews packed up their equipment, and the crowd began to melt away.

Steeg walked up to Gideon El. "Nice show."

"Good to see you again, Detective." His nose twitched from the sour smell that surrounded Steeg like a miasma. "Must have been one heck of a party."

Steeg ignored the dig. "How many of your gang actually lives here?"

"That's hardly the point now, is it? A life is a life, and when it's cruelly taken, the tragedy is that much greater."

"Very noble, and said with a straight face. But I still haven't figured out what's in it for you."

Gideon El smiled, revealing a set of beautifully capped teeth. "The greater good, Detective. The greater good."

CHAPTER NINETEEN

Dave's six-bedroom Colonial sat on two manicured acres at the top of the New Jersey Palisades. Steeg and Dave sat in a glass-enclosed porch, defiantly decorated in the bright shades of summer: white-painted walls, rattan furniture with thick cushions, and freshly cut flowers in expensive vases.

At 5:00 p.m the sun was nearly down. The sulfurous yellow dome of the sky slowly turned a matte black and appeared to flow into the Hudson. With the darkening, the city awakened. The river's eastern shore, south to the Battery, sparkled like a drift of fireflies, and Manhattan glowed, etching an aurora borealis in the sky.

After Herkie's funeral, Steeg decided that DeeDee needed a change of scenery and he needed to spend some time with his brother. He and DeeDee were on speaking terms again, but just barely. Two steps forward and one back. It was the story of his life.

Dave and Franny's oldest son, Anthony, was in the middle of his freshman year at Dartmouth. That left thirteen-year-old Angie and eleven-year-old Tommy to entertain DeeDee. From the sound of things, they were getting along pretty well.

Franny carried in a black lacquered tray with two steaming mugs of black coffee and a dish of Mallomars. She wrinkled her nose at the pall of blue smoke suspended in the air like marsh gas. She and Dave were a love story, childhood sweethearts whose devotion to each other was incorruptible. Steeg envied them. Her hips were a little wider now, the lines at the corners of her mouth a bit deeper, and her short butterscotch hair was showing a bit of gray, but Franny didn't concern herself with things like that.

She perched herself on Dave's knee, and he ran his hand under her beige turtleneck, lightly stroking her back.

"So, Jake, you seeing anyone?"

Franny's mission in life was to marry him off. She had set him up so many times, he had lost count. At first, the women were young and single. Now, they were divorced with kids.

He brought the cup to his lips. It was too hot. He put it down and reached for a Mallomar and popped it in his mouth. "Y'know, you can't get these in the summer. Has to do with the chocolate. Melts in the heat, so the stores don't stock them," Steeg said.

"I know," she said. "I buy a gross and freeze them. Now, let's get back to the question. Are you seeing anyone?"

"Nope."

"I've got a friend —"

Steeg cut her off. "I know. She's lovely, a good Catholic, two beautiful children, and an ex who's an asshole. That about right?"

Feigning anger, she shot to her feet. "Why do you have to be such a putz? I just want to see you as happy as we are."

"*We're* happy?" Dave said, pulling her onto his lap and planting a wet one on her lips. "Leave him alone. He's tried it and doesn't like it. *He's* happy."

She took a playful swipe at him. "Okay, I'm going to check on the kids and get dinner going, but if you change your mind, give me a call."

Dave waited until Franny left before he spoke. "I squared it with Jimmy Nolan."

"You heard."

"You ain't exactly a docile drunk. Said when you got finished, his place looked like you took a sledge to it. How're you feeling?"

"Like a screwup."

Dave nodded. "Anything I can do to help?"

"No. It's up to me. But while I was puking my guts up, I had your basic wet-brain revelation. Our Lady of the Tile Floor appeared to me and shared a bit of secret lore. She said that alcoholics are the arsonists of the soul. Not only our own, but the souls of everybody we touch. Profound, huh?"

"Gives me an erection just thinking about it."

"Make fun, see if I care, but I've had my last drink, Dave."

"Because of the revelation?"

"No, because of DeeDee."

"Sure," he said, unable to keep the skepticism out of his tone. "Speaking of church, did you go today?"

"You've got to be kidding."

"It's the anniversary of Mom's death. There was a Mass. I thought you'd remember."

Steeg did remember, but he dealt with it in a way that didn't include church. There was a time when he believed in an essential goodness, even when he was on the force. But priests buggering little kids finally convinced him that evil was more real and far more pervasive.

"A day doesn't go by that I don't think of her."

"That's something, at least." Dave was silent for a few moments. "He was stepping out on her, you know."

"What are you talking about? Who was stepping out?"

"Dominic, he was stepping out on her."

If Dave had told him that the family was really a nest of crypto-Jews it wouldn't have surprised him more.

"Dominic? Come on! The minute his shift ended, he came home. Where the hell did he find time?"

"He did."

"How do you know?"

"Some things you just know."

"Dave, I —"

Dave stroked the spot on his cheek where the port-wine stain had been. "Remember what he used to call me? Momma's boy. Something, huh? Momma's boy. I guess he was right. I could do no wrong in her eyes. If I were standing over a corpse with a smoking .38 in my hand, she'd say it wasn't me. Momma's boy," he spat. "Dominic was some piece of work. Wanted to toughen me up. The guy has ham hocks for hands. You got off easy. By the time he got done with me, he was too tired to go after you. If it wasn't for Mom, he'd a killed me." He tried to smile, but his face had turned to stone. "But that's all in the past, water under the bridge. Right?"

Steeg gazed out the window at a tug, its red and green running lights lit up like a Christmas tree, nosing a barge upstream. "We both know what he is, but I still don't believe he cheated on her."

"Fine, have it your way."

Suddenly, Dave brightened.

"So, what's going on in your life?"

Grateful that they were finally moving on, Steeg told him about Herkie.

"I remember him, the poetry guy. Damndest thing I ever saw. The guy's mind was filled with scrap metal, but he always delivered. Kind of like a whatdoyacallit, y'know, like the Rainman."

"Idiot savant."

"Right. You give 'em a date three thousand years ago and they'll tell you what day of the week it was."

"That wasn't Herkie, he was smart."

"No doubt, that's why he called a fuckin' shipping carton home."

Steeg felt the heat rise to his cheeks. "He was my friend."

Dave, more than anyone, understood the calculus of loyalty and realized he had gone too far. He took a deep drag on the cigar and slowly let the smoke out. "Fair enough. But what do you want from me?"

"The way I see it, he was in the wrong place at the wrong time."

"How so?"

"Let me play it out for you, just talk it through. A girl

is found dead in my neighbor's apartment. Turns out the neighbor has two jobs that I know of. He's running girls for Joey Rizzo and working for Mallus and Sloan at Hudson Democratic at the same time."

"And you know this how?"

"Herkie. Saw the neighbor pimping her in an alley outside Pinky's. The Sloan connection came from Luce, you remember her?"

"Your partner, the hot lesbian. How's she doing?"

"Fine."

"So that's why you got into Mallus's and Rizzo's face."

"You heard."

"Hard not to. I hear you were like a crazy man, making threats, going off."

"Maybe just a little."

"I used to think maybe it was the sauce that wound you up, and once you were off, I'd see a kinder, gentler Jake. Shows what I know. Anyway, keep going."

"And then I heard that the Department brass put a shadow on me. Like I'm screwing their pooch, too."

"And when you add it all up?"

"I get the feeling that I'm all alone in Indian country and there's an arrow with my name on it winging its way toward my chest."

"You want my opinion?"

"That's why I'm here."

"Okay, here goes. Mallus is a politician, he doesn't have the balls. Ditto with Terry. Joey Rizzo is another story. He has the balls, but he's a worker, he ain't paid to make decisions."

"What about Lenny Roberts, his boss?"

"A possibility, if you push too hard, but he doesn't know you from Adam's cat."

"Then who is it?"

"Let me think about it. Besides, I wouldn't let anything happen to you. You're all I've got. Y'know, family matters, and all that fuzzy shit."

CHAPTER TWENTY

To celebrate Luce and Cherise Adams's decision to marry, Steeg joined them at Daffodil, a trendy SoHo restaurant.

The brainchild of a celebrity chef who hosted a hit show on the Food Network, Daffodil was designed with an Art Deco look in mind: lots of intense colors, stainless steel, and geometrics. Unfortunately, the cuisine was designed the same way, like it had been constructed in metal shop. In an interesting twist, the kitchen sat on an island in the center of the dining room.

Steeg was in a sour mood, a leftover from his half gainer into the bottle of Jack Black. He threw a baleful glance at the kitchen.

"It's a rare treat to actually watch the cooks sweating into the food. Leaves nothing to the imagination."

"Y'know, I think I liked you better when you were drinkin'. For sure, you were a damned sight more fun."

"I suspect you're right."

"Look, I know you'd rather be eating slop out of a trough, but suck it up. I'm buyin' and I'd like to enjoy it. In other words, stop rainin' on our damned parade."

Cherise giggled. The three had been friends ever

since he and Luce had partnered up. Like Luce, Cherise
was tall and slim and a cop, but there, the resemblance
stopped. She had mocha skin, and a softly triangular face
that came to a rounded point at her chin.

"So, you're finally doing it. After the last breakup, I
thought it was over."

Cherise affectionately massaged a spot between
Luce's shoulder blades.

"So did we, until we realized that it didn't work for
us apart, so maybe the problem was that the 'together'
wasn't permanent."

Steeg lifted his glass of sparkling water.

"May you have better luck than I had."

Luce and Cherise lifted their champagne flutes and
clinked them against Steeg's glass.

"Set a date yet?"

"Baby steps, Steeg," Cherise said. "Baby steps."

"I heard about your friend," Cherise said. "I'm terribly sorry."

"Yeah, and then Gideon El shows up with his army
of trained seals and tries to make political hay. The guy
has no shame. No shame at all."

"Tell me about it. I remember him from the old days,
in Brooklyn. There was this high school in Bensonhurst
that had seen better days. When it was built in the forties,
the neighborhood was all Jews and Italians and everyone
got along pretty well. Then, it must have been the sixties,
the city put up this low-income project and bussin' came
in and the shit hit the fan. It was like a double whammy.
When Luce and I got to the Six-One in the early nineties, it
was Katie bar the door." She turned to Luce. "Remember?"

"Oh, yeah. The Jews started movin' out and the blacks and Italians recreated by kickin' the shit out of each other until they got tired of it and teamed up against the Asian kids. They must have figured it was an extracurricular activity, like biology club."

"And then Gideon El shows up, only he was the Reverend Randall Carver then, with lint in his pockets and a mail-order theology degree from some school he found on the back of a book of matches," Cherise said. "Blames the Asian kids. Says these nerdy little kids are beatin' on the blacks, and some people actually took him seriously! Can you believe it? There were maybe twelve of 'em in the whole school, skinny little things who hung out in the computer lab."

"Sounds like Randall," Steeg said.

"Don't it, though. The media jumped on it, and pretty soon the brother had him a new job title, 'Professional Activist,'" Luce said. "Why anyone with a brain stem buys his line of bullshit is beyond me. Hear he's goin' to make a run for mayor next time around." She shrugged. "Why the hell not? Seems like the logical next step."

"He said that a couple of homeless guys bought it in the last few weeks, sort of hinting at a possible serial killer," Steeg said.

"Could be, all the signs are there. Easy targets. Similar backgrounds. No one's gonna miss 'em. Happened before. Remember that gang of Rican kids up in the Bronx? Torched half a dozen or so street people before they were taken down."

Steeg remembered. "They were all juvies."

"Yep. Thirteen, fourteen. Sent 'em to a youth facility." She sighed. "Probably out now, walkin' with Jesus and workin' on their next shop of horrors. What a wonderful country!"

"I'm not buying it," Steeg said.

"Which part?"

"The serial killer theory." He reached into a metal basket for a piece of bread filled with nuts and some dark things he couldn't identify. It tasted like nutty cardboard. He set it down. "It just doesn't pass the smell test. Too many things going on."

"But it does pass the serial killer test. Once is an incident. Twice is a coincidence. Three times is a pattern. Look, I don't care what the motive is. We've had three homeless people killed in one neighborhood. Anyway, we've contacted the FBI and asked their profilers to take a look."

"Should hear from them in a year or so, and it's gonna be bullshit, anyway," Steeg said, familiar with the ways of the FBI.

"M.E. report came back on Herkie. .22 — matches the bullet we fished out of Moore. You got any ideas?"

Steeg studied his fingernails. "Too many."

CHAPTER TWENTY-ONE

The suspension had made Steeg sloppy, and it took Luce to make him realize it. His head was swimming with ideas and a bunch of other things he wasn't particularly proud of, and that was the problem. It was time to substitute resolve for moral weakness, time to take stock. At its most elemental level a murder investigation is a single-minded pursuit of the facts. Only then do the white spaces begin to give up their secrets. He had made the rookie mistake of being reactive, allowing events to wash over him. The first step was to figure out just exactly which murder he was investigating.

It had all started with one murder, Diana Strickland's, followed closely by Moore's and Herkie's. Linda Strickland — the one he was most interested in — made it a possible four.

DeeDee was at school and the apartment was quiet. He pulled a yellow legal-sized pad and a pencil out of the desk drawer in the living room, brewed a fresh pot of coffee, and settled in on the sofa.

Rain pattered softly against the windowpanes.

He divided the pad into four columns, and in small block letters headed each column with a victim's name.

He started with what he knew. The time for speculation would come later.

DIANA STRICKLAND. Murdered, 3/12/04, my apartment house. Cause of death: overdose. Rich kid gone off the tracks. Junkie hooker. Worked at Pinky's. "WHY?"

GRAHAM MOORE. Murdered roughly the same time as Diana. Cause of death: gunshot wound to the head. Lowlife. Worked for Albert Mallus, Terry Sloan. Pimped for Lenny Roberts and Joey Rizzo at Pinky's. "WHY?"

HERKIE. Murdered 3/18/04. Cause of death: bullet to the head. Same small-caliber gun that killed Moore. Outside of my apartment. Last person to see Diana alive. Saw her hooking. Knew Moore was her pimp. "WHY?"

LINDA STRICKLAND. Died 8/6/75. Cause of death: pushed or fell from terrace. Society lady. Wife of Earl, and mother of Diana and Caroline. Murder or suicide?

Still holding the pad, he went into the kitchen, poured the steaming coffee into a chipped green mug, and looked out the window. He set the pad down on the Formica table and took a sip of coffee, clearing his mind, letting everything settle in.

After a few minutes, he picked up the pad and studied it in the half-light. There had to be something linking these deaths, but he couldn't see it. A fruitless half-hour later, he threw on his coat, took the pad, and went down to the river to clear his head.

The pier was empty. A hard north wind kicked up whitecaps between floes of slow-moving pancake ice. Seabirds rode on their surface, heads turned into the wind, their beaks buried beneath their wings.

He pulled the collar of his jacket and studied his notes. It took a while, but a pattern, still indistinct, began to take form. Three things jumped out at him. Three murders committed in, or connected with, *his* apartment house. Two of the victims were from the same family. And last, Herkie and Moore were killed with the same gun. What did sleazebags like Roberts and Rizzo have to do with this? What about Sloan and Gideon El, both for sale to the highest bidder? Theories began to crystallize, but he shut them down, realizing that he was falling into the trap of flabby thinking again. This wasn't the time for theories, he reminded himself. He only knew parts. At the very least, Herkie's murder was intended to be a message for him. Why, he didn't know, but it made it personal and made him a potential target. The one thing he did know was that it was time to stop chasing thirty-year-old ghosts. From here on in, he decided, his focus would be Diana Strickland. Find her murderer and everything else would fall into place.

With that settled, he went back up to his apartment and called Caroline.

CHAPTER TWENTY-TWO

Steeg met Caroline inside the lobby of her father's building on Fifth and Fifty-ninth, overlooking Central Park. It was a prewar "old money" building faced in red brick that had weathered to a muddy brown. She was wearing a full-length, white-hooded coat made from the skins of an endangered species, a rust-colored, scoop-necked sweater, and black slacks tucked into knee-high black leather boots. Steeg, wearing a navy blue blazer, gray slacks, and black, tasseled loafers that he had ruined walking in the slush, felt decidedly underdressed.

"I was wondering whether I'd ever hear from you again," she said, leaning in for a kiss.

"I had an accident."

It caught her in mid-lean. "What happened?"

"I fell off the wagon."

She wasn't amused.

"A very old, very bad joke," Steeg said. "But sadly true."

"And now?"

He flashed a Boy Scout salute. "Pure of heart, mind, and body, and ready to take on the world." He paused. "I really appreciate you setting this up with your father."

"He's not well, but if it'll help you find the monster who hurt Diana . . ." Her voice trailed off into a whisper. "I still have a hard time understanding how she got into this mess."

An interesting way to put it, Steeg thought. "You never know where information leads."

"Are you ready to go up?"

"Yep."

"You're not going to like him, you know."

"Won't make a difference. The people I don't like can fill Yankee Stadium, one more won't matter. The real question is will he like me?"

Caroline took a step back and regarded him. "I don't think so. Few measure up to his exacting standards."

Steeg smiled. "Your father and I have a lot more in common than you think."

She took a deep breath. "Okay." She walked over to a doorman all decked out in a Gilbert & Sullivan uniform. He had a "retired cop" look: doughy faced, balding and going to fat. "George, please call Mr. Strickland and tell him we're on our way up."

George tipped the brim of his HMS *Pinafore* admiral's cap and picked up the phone.

The elevator opened on a foyer carpeted with a large Oriental rug woven in vibrating reds, yellows, and blues. As if on signal, the door to the apartment swung open. A man moving into the outer reaches of middle age, with soft features and thinning brown hair, wearing a white jacket a size too small, black pants, and white shirt with a bowtie, greeted them. He looked harried.

Caroline shrugged off her coat and handed it to him.

"Miss Caroline, so good to see you again."

"John I'd like you to meet a friend of mine, Steeg. Steeg, this is John Sayres."

"Mr. Steeg," John said, with a slight nod of his head. "May I take your coat?"

Steeg offered his hand instead. "How are you, John? Good to meet you."

John, apparently unaccustomed to the normal rituals of social intercourse in this household, seemed rattled by Steeg's gesture. Hesitating at first, he eventually took Steeg's hand and shook it with increasing vigor bordering on pleasure. Realizing that he had temporarily thrown poor John off-kilter, Steeg slipped out of his coat, folded it lengthwise and, with a wink, handed it to him.

John reddened, trying to suppress a smile.

"How's Daddy?" Caroline asked.

The mention of "Daddy" was enough to reinstate John's harried look.

"Not a particularly good day, Miss. He's in the library."

"Seems like a good guy," Steeg said, after John had left.

"He's been with Daddy since Diana and I were children. We had nannies, but they came and went. John managed to hang in."

"So, he knew your mother."

"Yes, he did."

Despite Steeg's vow not to chase ghosts, a conversation with John wouldn't hurt.

He followed Caroline into the living room. It looked like an *Architectural Digest* cover. The walls were covered in soft yellow silk. Oriental carpets of varying sizes and design sat on the floor surrounded by chairs and tables with inlays and impossibly slender legs. Bibliots straight out of *Antiques Roadshow* were everywhere. Through the French doors was the terrace, where dead plants poked out of snow-coned terra-cotta pots, and beyond that was Central Park.

His apartment would have made a fair-sized walk-in closet in this layout, Steeg thought.

"You grew up here?"

"Sure, just your normal fifteen-room apartment in Gotham."

"Now I know what I want to be in my next life."

"Be careful what you wish for. The library is through here," she said, taking his hand and leading him down a hallway past closed doors to another room, not as spacious but just as breathtaking in its own way.

A floral-patterned Tiffany lamp that was worth more than Steeg's pension cast a dim, orangey glow over the room. It sat on an end table next to a leather sofa the color of dark butter. From floor to ceiling the walls were lined with books, many bound in leather. A wooden rail circled the shelves. A ladder matching the color of the dark wood paneling leaned against the rail.

Without realizing it, Steeg reached out to the shelf nearest him and ran his hand along the spines of the books.

"You like books?" The feathery voice coming from the sofa sounded like it had been shaped in ossified lungs.

Steeg pulled his hand back as if it had touched something hot. "Yes sir, I do."

Earl Strickland, wearing what Steeg guessed was a

maroon smoking jacket bound at the waist by a similar colored sash, dragged himself to his feet. A clear tube clipped to his septum led to an oxygen tank standing between the arm of the sofa and the end table.

Strickland was tall and gaunt, about Steeg's size. He had thin, colorless lips and eyes the color of washed-out denim. His hair was gray and wispy. The bridge of his nose was saddled and veered off slightly at the tip, giving him a pugnacious look.

"My wife liked books, too." His voice sounded wistful, but then it hardened. "My daughters are another story." He slumped back onto the sofa, as if the effort of speaking had cost him more than he could afford.

Caroline walked over and took his hand. "How're you feeling?"

"Like the Philistines when Samson pulled the damned roof down on them." He turned his attention to Steeg. "Come closer so I can see you. Eyes are starting to go."

"Daddy, this is Steeg."

He reached for Strickland's hand. It had the desiccated feel of an insect wing. "Good to meet you, sir."

Strickland nodded in an offhanded way, but his eyes measured Steeg carefully. "You know the only reason I'm talking to you is because Caroline asked."

"I appreciate that."

"Do you need me, sir?" John was at the doorway.

Irritated at the interruption, Strickland swung his head around. "Did I ring?" he snapped.

John's cheeks colored. He lowered his head and backed out of the room.

Caroline was right, Steeg didn't like him. Earl Strickland was a man of piteous gifts whose pilot light had gone out a long time ago. Now he drew warmth by stripping the dignity and honor from others and validation from their humiliation.

"So, you like books, eh? Who's your favorite fictional character, Mr. Steeg?"

Steeg nearly blurted out, "Snoopy," but from the man's tone he knew that Earl Strickland wasn't given to idle questions. There was a point to this exercise, and it was all about intimidation — the droit du seigneur that was his right by birth, circumstance, and the number of zeros in his bankbook.

Fine, Steeg thought. If the asshole wants to play, we'll play.

"I guess I'd have to say, Inspector Javert."

Strickland smiled, warming to the prospect of making Steeg look stupid. "And why is that?"

Steeg's lips curled into a tight smile, and he fixed him with his eyes. "He was a good cop who never quit. Even with all his money, Jean Valjean had to sleep with one eye open."

Strickland's jaw went slack, and in the orangey glow his face took on a sickly cast.

Steeg had scored a direct hit — on what, he didn't know — but there was no question he had blown Strickland's little game into scrap.

Sensing a distinct change in the temperature, Caroline broke in. "Perhaps we'd better get to the reason why Steeg is here."

Strickland's gaze lingered on Steeg for a few seconds, reappraising him, before breaking off. His tone changed, allowing grief to creep in. "Of course, poor Diana. Take a seat, Mr. Steeg. Caroline."

She lowered herself onto a cushion next to her father. Steeg took a seat across from them, in a chair with impossibly slender legs and arms, feeling incredibly cramped.

"Tell me about Diana, Mr. Strickland."

"Diana." He sighed, looking directly at Caroline for confirmation and support. "A headstrong, destructive, unhappy child. Unpredictable. Hard to know which Diana would show up at any given time."

Caroline sat very still, her gaze focused on the hands clasped in her lap.

Strickland continued. "Everything we did for her came to naught and wound up in an ugly *scene*. I often wondered if she were a changeling. I must confess that her mother was far more forgiving than I."

"That's not totally true," Caroline said, her gaze still fastened on her lap. "She was a sweet child. It was only witnessing that . . . that horrible *thing* that she began to act up." Caroline's voice was small and floated in the air.

"What horrible thing?" Steeg said.

"Diana saw her mother being murdered."

Now that is new news, Steeg thought. It certainly wasn't in any report he'd read. "Was this reported to the police?"

Two red spots the size of radishes appeared on Strickland's cheeks. His breathing became even more labored.

"Of course not. A figment of a frightened child's

imagination. Never proved," he rasped. "She was in therapy for years, and what good did it do? Truancy, theft,
selling her body, cavorting with that ridiculous Stepin
Fetchit black man, and disgracing my name."

For the first time, Caroline looked directly at him,
her face a question mark.

"Yes," he said. "I know all about it. That's why I
hired a private detective to find her." His voice took on a
conspiratorial tone. "He found out."

Steeg leaned forward but kept his mouth shut, Caroline was doing a pretty good job on her own.

Her voice was barely a whisper. "Found out what,
Daddy?"

The red tint darkened to scarlet and spread over
Strickland's face. His chest heaved with a coughing
spasm.

"John," he called. "I . . . need your . . . assistance."

"Found out *what*, Daddy?" Caroline repeated, her
voice rising.

Sayres appeared and rushed to the oxygen tank, ad-
justing the valve to increase the flow. He turned to Steeg
and Caroline. "I'm afraid you'll have to leave now."

"Not before I get an answer." Caroline's voice was
cold steel. "Found . . . out . . . what?"

"She was sleeping with him. That . . . minstrel act!"
He paused to catch his breath and then spat the name
out. "Gideon El."

CHAPTER TWENTY-THREE

Steeg left Caroline and her father to tiptoe through the twisted, pointy edges of their own barbed wire, and he had another suspect to consider. Gideon El. The man definitely gets around, he thought. What would he want with a junkie prostitute, he wondered? Sex? He could do much better, unless his tastes ran to back alley quickies. Or did their relationship begin before she'd opted to work in the meat market? Was she blackmailing him? Possibly. At the very least, it supplied motive. It would also explain why Moore was picked as her executioner. Gideon might have shared his problem with Rizzo, or even Terry Sloan, and Moore, an expendable lowlife who worked for both men, was given the assignment. But Steeg knew he was getting ahead of himself. He reminded himself again that at this point he only knew parts. At the corner of Fifth and Fifty-eighth he stopped to wait for the light to change. The sun had come out, warming the air several degrees.

"Mr. Steeg, Mr. *Steeg!*"

He turned and saw Sayres chugging toward him. From the looks of him, it was the first time he had stepped it up from a brisk walk. By the time he reached Steeg, he was blowing hard.

"I'm . . . glad I found . . . you. George wasn't terribly . . . sure which way you went."

"Settle down, John. Wouldn't want you to stroke out on me."

Sayres bent over at the waist, palms on his thighs, trying to get his pulse rate below 2,000. His skin was the color of tallow.

"I don't have much time," he wheezed. "I put him to bed and told Caroline that I need to get one of his prescriptions filled."

"I've got a question. What's it like working for someone with the charm of a pit viper?"

He looked up and managed a shrug. "One does what one must to survive. I must have a word with you, it's important."

Steeg glanced across the street. "Sure. How's about we get off the tundra into someplace warm?"

"We could go into the lobby of the General Motors Building. It's right here."

Steeg had a better idea. The time spent with Strickland had made him feel depressed and dirty. He needed his spirits lifted.

"Or we could go to the Plaza," he said.

Sayres looked across the street, past the bronze Pulitzer Fountain, at one of the premier hotels in the world. He gestured at his uniform. "Oh no, I'm not dressed for it."

Steeg pulled off his necktie and jammed it into his jacket pocket. "Neither am I."

He steered Sayres across Fifth, and they climbed the steps to the main entrance into the square, marble-walled lobby. The fresh-cut flowers, lush carpets, burnished brass, and gilded ceilings did the trick. Steeg felt instantly renewed.

"Let's have a drink," he said, steering Sayres toward the Palm Court.

Sayres held back.

"I don't think it would be appro —"

"We're bonding, John, and I can't think of a better place."

The large room had the antiseptic smell of a hotel and the acoustics to insure privacy.

They found a table close by a mirrored wall. Sayres ordered a vodka and tonic, and Steeg a cup of coffee.

"Okay, John, what's on your mind?" Steeg said.

Sayres seemed jumpy, swiveling his head around every few minutes as if expecting Strickland to come charging in at any moment and haul him out by the scruff of his neck.

Their drinks came. Steeg emptied four packets of sugar into his cup, stirring it around until it formed a gritty sludge at the bottom of the cup. His craving for sugar was inversely proportional to his withdrawal from alcohol. John tipped the vodka and tonic to his lips and nearly drained the glass.

Steeg recognized a brother in arms, a fellow member of the Fraternity of the Bottle. It was easy to see how working for Earl Strickland could have that effect on people.

Sayres looked at the inch or so of liquid in his glass

with something bordering on lust. Steeg didn't offer a re-fill; he wanted him focused on the moment.

Sayres seemed to sense Steeg's intentions. With the back of his fingers, he slid the glass off the napkin and pushed it to the side.

"This is difficult, so bear with me, please."

Steeg nodded. "Take your time."

John fiddled with the napkin, folding it double with great precision and then double again, repeating the process until it was the size of a postage stamp.

"It's not my habit to gossip about my employer or pry into his life, but in this case, I can hold my tongue no longer." He paused. "I overheard your conversation. Mr. Strickland reciting all that he had done for Diana. He certainly did, but it wasn't what he told you. He drove her out, you know," he said, carefully unfolding the napkin and smoothing it out.

"Who drove who out?"

"Mr. Strickland. Drove Diana out." He looked at Steeg. "If it's all right with you, I'd like a refill."

"Do you think that's a good idea?"

John reached into his jacket pocket and retrieved a tin of Altoids and a breath spray. "Cures all ills. Surely a man with a craving for sweets understands." He threw Steeg a knowing look. "The sugar helps, Mr. Steeg, but the need never goes away."

"Now I know why I like you, John," he said, signaling to the waiter for a refill. "Tell me about the Great Man."

"Inherited wealth, impulsive, brains of a hand puppet, never earned a dime himself. Earl Junior's father took one look at his son and fully expected shirtsleeves to shirtsleeves in two generations. He was not about to let that happen. He surrounded him with a cadre of smart people who actually ran the business. I suspect Earl Junior found it a bit disconcerting. All dressed up and nowhere to go, in a manner of speaking. His role at the company was, and is, purely ceremonial. Even the stock is controlled by a trust."

Their drinks arrived.

"Earl Junior caused a major rift when he married Mrs. Strickland. I daresay it was his first and last rebellious act."

"Why's that?"

Realizing that this might be his last drink for a while, John forced himself to take it in small sips. "She was a fashion model, featured in magazines, but she wasn't *known*. Appeared out of nowhere. Didn't travel in the Stricklands' circles. No parents, no relatives, and, yet, much too decent for the Stricklands. They didn't know what to make of her." He paused. "And, worst of all, they couldn't control her."

"What was she like?"

"Warm, generous, loving." He gazed out into the lobby. "I know that it sounds trite, but she was the morning sun and the evening star."

"It sounds as if you loved her."

"Loved her? Yes, it was impossible not to. In love, no, I'm not wired that way." He blushed. "She's the reason I stayed. After her death, I should have left, but someone had to protect the children."

"From?"

"Mr. Strickland."

The direction the conversation was heading was making Steeg uncomfortable.

"It turned out that it was Diana who needed me more," Sayres continued. "For some reason, Caroline was never the subject of his attention."

"And Diana was?"

He nodded. "It began several months after Mrs. Strickland's death."

Steeg sat quietly, waiting for the other shoe to drop.

Sayres lifted the glass to his lips and gulped the contents down. "The nightly visits to Diana's bedroom."

The flame in Steeg's dark place began to flicker, making the snakes restive.

"If you stayed to protect the children, you did a pretty piss-poor job."

"*No!* I did as much as I could. My job was to tend to Mr. Strickland's comfort. The children were the nannies' responsibility. They knew what he was doing and quit."

"Why didn't they report him to the police?"

"They knew the consequences: a one-way ticket back to Third World hell. Who could blame them? They had their own families to support. No, there was no help there. The last nanny, a woman named Alma Gonzalez, informed me of her suspicions before she left. At first I refused to believe her, but in time I saw the truth. Only Diana, never Caroline. It struck me as odd, but I'm not an expert in these matters. With Alma's departure, care of the children was added to my responsibilities, and I saw things firsthand."

Steeg's knuckles were chalk white. "Did Caroline know?"

"Not unless Diana told her, and I doubt that she did. At least, Caroline never mentioned it to me."

John continued. "The poor child suffered night-mares, panic attacks, unexplained outbursts of anger, bed-wetting. Mr. Strickland's nocturnal visits–'to comfort her,' he claimed — only exacerbated her condition."

"And you stood by and watched?"

He slammed his fist on the table. "*No,* again! I confronted him, informed him of my suspicions, and demanded that he stop or I would go to the authorities."

"Did he?"

"It was quite a scene. He accused *me* of fabricating a monstrous lie and threatened me with dismissal and worse."

"Seems like a small price to pay."

"For you, perhaps. Mr. Strickland is an evil, vindictive man with many resources. He had dredged up something in my past, something I'm not particularly proud of. He told me that his attorneys would see to it that *I* would be labeled a pedophile and the perpetrator of the crime against his child. He reminded me that prison is not a happy experience for men carrying the child-molester label."

He lifted his glass, scooped an ice cube out with his finger, popped it in his mouth, and sucked at it hungrily, but it offered neither relief nor absolution.

Child molesters occupied the bottom rung of the prison food chain. Convicts with the ambient noise of demons chittering in their heads used pedophiles in ways that beggared the imagination.

"He blackmailed you."

"It was more like a Mexican standoff. We each had something on the other. I did exact one concession, though. I insisted that a psychiatrist treat Diana. Reluctantly, he agreed."

"That was Dr. Weldon."

"Correct. Sheila Weldon, psychiatrist to the rich. Bought and paid for. As soon as Diana started treatment, I called Weldon. Requesting anonymity, I provided as complete a picture of the family situation as I could. Weldon's response was to turn Diana into a medicated zombie." He gave his head a rueful shake. "So much for medical ethics."

"Why are you telling me this now, when he could still hurt you?"

Without seeking Steeg's permission, John signaled the waiter for a refill.

"Not anymore. My pact with the Devil is null and void." He smiled a sad smile. "I've been diagnosed with pancreatic cancer. I won't see the summer."

Steeg suddenly felt a weariness that sapped thought from his brain and the marrow from his bones. "Is there anything I can do?"

"Make him pay, Mr. Steeg. Make him pay."

CHAPTER TWENTY-FOUR

Steeg sensed that he was being followed. By the time he reached Joe Allen, a theater district restaurant on Forty-sixth between Eighth and Ninth, he was sure. His tail was as discreet as a garbage truck, and never more than twenty yards behind. He was either sloppy, uncommonly stupid, or wanted Steeg to know that he was there. Either way, Steeg didn't take kindly to the intrusion. The man appeared to have been carved from a block of hard wood. With coppery skin the texture of burlap stretched tight on the planes of his face, he looked as if he had just stepped out of a Remington painting. A warrior. His chest was as wide as a barrel, and his long, glossy black hair was pulled tight in a ponytail looped through the back of a Redskins cap. The camouflage jacket and jeans he wore barely contained him.

Steeg paused several times and waited for him to catch up, but he didn't oblige, continuing to hang back. Tiring of the game, Steeg turned and walked up to him. "Is there something on your mind, pal?" Steeg said.

The Indian appeared nonplussed. "Many things good and hurtful, things that try my soul, but why would that be of interest to you, sir?"

The accent was Deep South, languorous and mossy, redolent of sun-dappled red dirt and shadowy rhododendron forests, with just enough lethal craziness to balance it all out.

"For the last ten blocks we've been tethered to each other, and frankly, it's annoying."

He flashed Steeg a half-mocking smile. "Two people make a busy road, and that's just the way it is."

Perfect, Steeg thought, the guy speaks in tongues.

"Let's cut the bullshit — who sent you?"

"The good Lord cuts a path in the wilderness for all of his children. I'm just followin' mine."

Steeg moved closer, his face inches from the Indian's. Three blue tears were tattooed under his right eye. Prison markings. A tear for each man he had killed. His breath smelled fetid, like something had died.

"I think it's time for you to take a new path. Am I making myself clear here?"

"Yessiree, boss, crystal clear." He raised his hands, palms out. "Don't want no trouble. I can plainly see that you're a man who don't brook nonsense from man or beast." He paused to reflect, and then his face lit up with a shining madness. "But what if the Lord Jesus wants me back on the road he mapped out?"

"You're gonna have to take it up with Him. Look, as much as I'm enjoying the time we've had together, I have to go now and I don't want to see you again. Understood?"

"Yessirree, boss. You go on your way and I'll go on mine. God be with you!"

Steeg turned and walked away. Halfway down the block, he looked back. The Indian was gone.

When he reached Forty-eighth Street, he stopped cold. Workmen were hammering plywood scaffolding along the entire north side of the street. Sal Matarazzo, wearing a T-shirt and tomato sauce–stained apron, stood outside his pizzeria, watching the boards go up. His arms looked like legs of lamb.

"What's going on?" Steeg said.

"I'm truly fucked. They canceled my lease."

"Didn't you just sign a renewal?"

"Like it fuckin' matters. Told me to shove it up my ass."

"Who told you?"

"New owners, something called Twenty-first Century Realty. The fuckin' work gang shows up this morning and they start unloadin' plywood sheets from a couple of flatbeds. By the time I get here at nine, they got the whole length of the block framed out. I'm steamin'. I go up to one of the jack-offs and ask for the head jack-off. He points out a guy looks like a Bartlett pear. Has a clipboard in his hand. I go up to him all pleasant-like and say what the fuck are you doin'? He asks my name and goes to his clipboard. There's a notice with my name on it. It's an eviction from the new owners. I crumple it up and throw it at him. I tell him to shove it up his ass. The mook laughs in my face. Tells me he's got enough copies to paper a shithouse."

"What did you do?"

"What any reasonable person would do. I grabbed the clipboard, then I grabbed him and tried to shove the clipboard up *his* ass!"

Steeg laughed. "How far did you get?"

"Let's put it this way, I don't thing he's gonna be doin' much ballroom dancin' for a while." His face collapsed in on itself as if the ignominy of his circumstances had robbed it of all moral and physical support. "What the fuck am I gonna do, Steeg? I got my whole life tied up in this joint."

"What does your lawyer say?"

"Find a new location, the cocksucker."

"How long do you have?"

"They gave me a month. Been here twenty-five years, and they give me thirty days. Pretty decent of them, huh?"

Steeg threw his arm over Sal's shoulder. "Anything you need, just ask."

"You're next — you know that, don't ya. They ain't gonna stop with me. You can bet the farm on it."

With that happy thought ringing in his head, Steeg climbed the stairs to his apartment. The wind off the river smelled of rotting fish and diesel oil.

The door frame was splintered, and the door slightly ajar. DeeDee was his first thought, but a quick glance at his watch told him that she was still at school. Relieved, he waited quietly, listening. After a few moments, he swung the door open.

The apartment had been trashed. The furniture was upended, drawers emptied, photos ripped from frames, CDs ground underfoot, cabinets tipped over and their contents strewn about like confetti. Whoever had violated his home had an interesting sense of humor: a mound of feces sat in the middle of DeeDee's bed.

Steeg knew that this wasn't the work of a shit-for-brains junkie looking to score something to fence. This was the work of a hardcase, a man with hornets in his brainpan and worms crawling through his veins.

Gathering the sheets up, Steeg happened to glance out of the window. The Indian stood across the street, looking up. His eyes were chunks of obsidian, swallowing the afternoon light. Smiling, he pointed his hand at Steeg, extended his index finger and made a gun of his fist. His mouth moved. Steeg couldn't hear him, but there was no mistaking the word his lips had formed.

"Bang!"

CHAPTER TWENTY-FIVE

"Your stuff was looking kind of ratty, anyway," DeeDee said, putting a good face on the situation. "By the way, why is my mattress sitting out in the street?"

"Out with the old, in with the new," Steeg said.

"How about a water bed, then?"

"In your next life, maybe. I called the mattress company. They'll be delivering a new one in a couple of hours." He reached into his pocket and brought out a twenty. "How's about you and Cherise go down to Sal's and bring back a pie. Sausage and extra cheese."

"You mean, you're letting me out of jail?"

"Something like that."

With the exception of his latest bender, things had been going pretty well between him and DeeDee. They had settled into a routine that seemed to work pretty well — school, dinner, homework, and plenty of freedom for both of them. Now, with the Indian hot on his trail, and his apartment recently trashed, all bets were off. DeeDee had become an unforeseen complication and had to be kept on a short leash. He called Luce, told her what had happened, and a half hour later, she and Cherise were in his apartment.

Luce waited until DeeDee and Cherise were gone before she spoke.

"Some kind of angry people. They really did a job, didn't they?" Luce said.

Steeg and DeeDee had straightened the apartment up, but it still looked like the Golden Horde had passed through. "Looks like a trip to IKEA is in order."

"Somethin' else is in order," Luce said, handing him a brown paper bag.

"What's this?"

"I think you'll need it. A compact Beretta. Handles .357 SIGs or 9 mm parabellums. Right now you got the SIGs."

"This thing could bring down an elk, or a rather large Indian," Steeg said, hefting it in his hand.

"That's the idea. You wing him with this, and his shoulder falls off. Kinda hard to do some payback when you're learning to eat with your left hand. I also got you a cell phone. The number is taped on the back. I know you hate them, but it's time."

"There goes my privacy. Now people can bother me whenever they want."

"That's the point, Jackson."

"I owe you," he said, turning the phone on and slipping it in his pocket.

"Bet your ass."

"He didn't have a chin," Steeg said.

"Who?"

"The Indian."

"Must be hard eatin' when you're shovelin' food in

your mouth and most of it tends to drop in your lap. Restaurant goers tend to notice things like that," Luce said.

"He had a chin, but there wasn't much to it, like it receded into his neck."

"Like the British royal family. Two more generations, and they'll be havin' that same restaurant problem."

"Probably going to have to feed them through tubes," Steeg said.

"So, here's what I've been thinking," Luce said. "So far, the bad guys are doin' things *around* you. Herkie and now your apartment."

"An escalating warning."

"Right. If DeeDee were here, there's no tellin' what might have gone down. The way I see it, you've got two choices. You can walk away from it, which you ain't gonna do, or somebody's gonna have to watch your back and DeeDee's. I talked to Cherise. We've both got some time comin' and can't think of a better place to spend it than here in the Kitchen. Waterfront view, if you use your imagination. Wake up every morning to the smell of raw sewage. God's little acre. A little slice of paradise."

"You'd do that?"

"Wouldn't you do it for me?"

In a heartbeat, he thought. "What do you have in mind?"

"Cherise and I take turns hangin' with DeeDee, leavin' you free to deal some serious 'get back,' if you catch my drift."

"Sounds like a plan."

"Now that that's settled, where do you go from here?"

"Have Frick and Frack come up with anything?"

"Gangemi and Swartz? *Please!* They're still runnin' a background check on Moore."

"Figures. Listen, if you have a minute, I'd like to talk it out with you."

She took a seat on the sofa. Steeg remained standing.

"What are friends for?"

He filled her in on his meetings with Earl Strickland and John Sayres.

"It's pretty confusing. Until Earl threw Gideon El into the mix, I thought he looked pretty good. Incest. Fear of exposure. The whole nine yards. Just your average American family. But why would he tell me that he sicced a P.I. on Diana? Hell, if he wanted to keep it neat, the P.I. has an unfortunate accident and so does Diana."

"With his money, he could make it happen and walk away clean."

"Exactly. As far as I know, he wasn't even aware of Moore."

"Maybe he's smarter than you think and he's tryin' to throw you off with Gideon El."

Steeg paced the length of the living room.

"Not according to Sayres, who described him as the dumbest white man in the galaxy. No, Strickland is a straight-ahead guy who doesn't know the meaning of the word 'canny.' "

"Which brings us to Gideon El."

"Right. What did Diana have on him?"

"The obvious. One phone call to the *Post* could get

him plastered all over Page Six and wreck his so-called political career."

"It didn't hurt Jesse Jackson when his indiscretions hit the news," Steeg said.

"His sweetie wasn't a junkie hooker."

"The only problem with that theory is that Jesse could have talked his way out of it if he wasn't staring down both barrels of a DNA paternity test. Gideon El didn't have that problem with Diana. What was Diana going to claim, that Gideon El was doing a skank? Most people figure that water seeks its own level, so how would she have hurt him?"

Luce shifted in her seat. "Where did that child go for a pizza, Rome? I'm gettin' kind of hungry."

"Check the fridge, there's probably something there."

"I did. Unfortunately, moldy cheese ain't on my diet. So, you're rulin' Gideon El out."

He took a seat next to Luce. "Not at all. Because he doesn't fit into the neat little box I created doesn't mean he didn't do it. Oh no, old Gideon El is still number one on my hit parade until someone else knocks him off. What if —"

A loud knock on the door cut Steeg off. He reached into the bag and took the Beretta out. Luce reached under her jacket and undid the snap of her holster.

Luce silently mouthed a question. "DeeDee?"

Steeg shook his head and motioned Luce to the far wall and he assumed a firing stance directly in front of the door.

"Yeah?"

The doorknob turned.

Steeg clicked the safety off and moved a few steps to the side. His finger tightened on the trigger.

"It's your father. Open up."

Luce threw Steeg a questioning look.

Just to be on the safe side, Steeg sidled up to the door and looked through the peephole.

Dominic stared back at him.

Steeg nodded to Luce and slipped the Beretta in his pocket. He unlocked the door and opened it.

Dominic, disheveled and bleary-eyed, took a quick look around. He reeked of alcohol "What the hell happened?"

Steeg stepped back. "Getting a jump on spring cleaning. What brings you here?"

"Can I come in?"

"Sure."

Dominic walked in with the rolling, unsteady gait of a sailor who had spent too long at sea.

"You had a break-in," he said, slurring his words. "Fuckin' neighborhood is goin' to the dogs!" He looked around until his gaze settled on Luce. "Your new girlfriend?" His tone was accusative and deprecatory.

"The friend part is right, *Detective* Luce Guidry. Luce, this is my father, Dominic Steeg."

Luce returned Dominic's iciness with a dollop of her own. "A pleasure," she said, not meaning a word of it.

"Junkies," Dominic said, looking around the apartment. "Just like cockroaches. They do their business when no one's around. In my day —"

Steeg cut him off. "This is the first time you've been here in a couple of years."

Dominic plopped down on the sofa and tried to focus. The tiny red blood vessels in his nose and cheeks resembled a map of the Interstate Highway System.

"You got a beer?"

"Fresh out," Steeg said.

"It figures. Anyway, you came to see me and now I'm returning the favor. Y'know, let bygones be bygones."

Steeg didn't believe him. Dominic's grudges were biblical, assigning blame to the thousandth generation.

"Great! How's about I get Dave up here and we have an old-time family reunion?"

"Better he wasn't born."

"I guess I should hold the call to the caterer."

Dominic flapped his hand in disgust. "You always had a mouth on you, didn't you? Your brother uses his fists, and you use your mouth. Both cut from the same chunk. No difference. Hurts just the same."

Steeg was embarrassed that they were airing their laundry in front of Luce. But along with embarrassment came contrition. For the first time in memory, Dominic's veil had parted, allowing actual feelings to show through.

"Look, I'm sorry. It's just —"

"I know," Dominic said. "I'm pushing all the wrong buttons. Story of my life. Look, all I want to know is how're you doing on the Strickland investigation. You came by asking questions, remember?"

"The daughter or her mother?"

"Each one, both, what the hell difference does it make?" he snapped. The old Dominic was back.

"I'm making progress with the daughter's murder. Her mother's a different story. I don't know zip."

"Is her husband still living?"

"Earl? Yeah, I met him."

"Me too. What did you make of him?"

"The Prince of Darkness."

"Yeah. I wonder what Linda ever saw in him. Beyond the money, of course." His voice was dreamy and far away, as if recalling a distant memory.

Dominic's use of Linda Strickland's given name struck a strangely discordant note. "You knew her?"

Dominic's eyelids fluttered like butterfly wings. "You know how it is. During an investigation you learn so much about the vic, you think you know them intimately. You become almost like friends."

His answer didn't entirely satisfy.

"For now, I'm concentrating on her daughter Diana," Steeg said. He went over to an end table, picked up a photograph of Diana off a pile, and handed it to Dominic. "I've been passing these out to people. You never know who saw or heard what, right?"

Dominic stared at the photo. "Pretty girl. Just like her mother." He paused. "Can you tell me about her?"

Steeg was distracted by the sound of a key scraping in the lock. The door swung open, and DeeDee swept in with the pizza. Steam curled through the vents in the green and red box.

"Sal wouldn't take your money," she announced.

"Here, baby," Luce said, taking the box from DeeDee. "Let's take it into the kitchen."

"That's all right," Steeg said. He turned to Dominic. "This is DeeDee Santos. DeeDee, this is my father."

She nodded a shy hello. "You want a slice? I got a large."

Dominic heaved himself to his feet. "I gotta go."

"Come on and join us, Pop."

Dominic shook his head. "Nah, gotta go. Another time."

He left, still holding Diana's picture.

The telephone rang. DeeDee picked it up.

"It's for you, Steeg. Somebody named Mallus," she said.

CHAPTER TWENTY-SIX

In the interest of privacy, Mallus and Sloan wanted to meet Steeg at Pier 86. In the interest of remaining alive, Steeg wanted to meet them someplace more public. He didn't know for sure that Mallus and Sloan had arranged for the Indian to hang his scalp from his saddle horn, but he wasn't taking any chances. They settled for Hudson Democratic. A murder at the club would be a downer for Sloan's upcoming congressional race.

Sloan's office was decorated in dark woods and somber tones befitting a political up-and-comer. One wall was a kind of Terry Sloan Wall of Honor. It was entirely dedicated to plaques and photos, all in engaging poses, of the upward trajectory of his life, the powerful men he knew, and the manifold good works he had accomplished along the way. Mother Teresa had nothing on him.

In sharp contrast, Sloan sat stiffly behind his desk. Gideon El sat just as stiffly on the sofa. They didn't look happy.

"You're pissing in the punch, Steeg," Mallus said, before the proper greetings could be exchanged. He looked at Steeg the way a piranha looks at dinner.

"My, but that's an interesting image," Steeg said. "You're quite the wordsmith, Albert."

"Climb down off your smart-ass horse for once, will ya?"

"'Smart-ass horse'? That's two in a row — are you gonna try for the never attempted three?"

Gideon El shook his head in dismay, while Sloan merely shook his head. Meanwhile, Mallus was turning a cherry pink.

"What's your problem, Steeg?" Mallus said.

"Call me a silly goose, but I don't fancy being prey."

"What are you talking about?"

"There's an Indian out there with the temperament of a flamethrower whose mission in life is to hang my scalp from his belt. Let's just say I don't appreciate it."

Sloan, Gideon El, and Mallus exchanged looks. Mallus was the first to speak.

"What kind of Indian are we talking about, here — a dot head or the wahoo kind?"

"Very politically correct, Albert. Really got your finger on the pulse of the city. No wonder you're the power behind the throne."

Mallus's pink color went direct to mauve without passing through strawberry.

"You're thinking we put a *hit* on you?" Sloan said.

"Can't think of any other candidates."

"And why would we do that?" Gideon El said.

"The Bard of Hell's Kitchen just said it. I'm pissing in the punch."

"We've got a serious disconnect here," Sloan said.

I've known you since we were kids, you're Dave's brother — why would I want you dead?"

Steeg opened his mouth to speak, but Sloan cut him off.

"Yeah, yeah, I know, you're pissing in the punch."

"Took the words right out of my mouth," Steeg said. "As for your other point, let's not forget that Tony Soprano killed his cousin."

"That was a damn television show," Mallus said, clearly losing patience.

"Right. And art imitates life, or is it the other way around? I never get it right."

"Enough!" Sloan said, bringing the flat of his hand down on his desk with enough force to make his CYO baseball trophy leap a foot in the air. "I don't know anything about any Indians, but you have my word that no one in this room ordered a hit on you. Satisfied?"

"Sure." Steeg turned his gaze toward Gideon El. "But does that include your late girlfriend?"

Purple shadows filtered through the window, casting an unhealthy glow on Gideon El's face.

"What girlfriend?" Gideon El said.

"Diana Strickland. How quickly we forget the wages of sin."

Gideon El tried to hide his discomfort in a way that made him appear even more uncomfortable.

"This is ridiculous. I never even met her," he said, looking to Sloan and Mallus for support.

"That's funny. Seems there's a P.I. says that you have."

"A P.I.?"

"Earl Strickland hired him to keep tabs on his daughter, and for some reason you showed up in his report."

"And you know this how?"

"He told me. I have a copy of the report, if you'd like to see it."

It was a small lie, but it immeasurably boosted Steeg's credibility rating.

Gideon El looked again to Sloan and Mallus for support, but Sloan was busy repositioning his CYO trophy, a process Mallus found endlessly fascinating.

"She was hardly a girlfriend," Gideon El said.

"More like your friendly neighborhood pump?"

"That's a crude way of putting it."

"I'm a crude kind of guy."

"Time out here," Sloan said, riding to the rescue. Gideon El nearly wept with relief.

"Everything can be explained, and it's the truth, but it all gets back to you, Steeg, and the distorted way you see things."

Steeg wasn't too sure about the "truth" part. "So, undistort me."

Sloan turned to Mallus. "Go get it, Al."

Mallus tapped a wall panel and a door opened.

"Just like in the movies," Steeg said.

Mallus ignored him. He brought out something covered with a black cloth, measuring roughly two feet by three feet. Sloan took it from him and set it on his desk.

"You know what this is?" Sloan said.

Steeg clapped his fists together. "Golly gee, magic tricks! There's a rabbit under there and you're gonna make it disappear."

"It's the future, asshole. And you're fucking it up."

With a dramatic flourish, Sloan pulled off the cloth, revealing an architect's model. The base was a broad plaza featuring a swirling stainless-steel fountain in the middle. Three circular buildings of varying heights, looking remarkably like kitchen canisters, soared up from the plaza floor. Tiny people sat on tree-shrouded benches scattered around the fountain.

"What do you think?" Sloan said.

Steeg didn't know what to think, so he said the first thing that popped into his head. "Hmm."

"This is Riverview," Sloan said, barely able to contain his excitement.

"Catchy."

"You really think so?"

"Not really. And this is going where?"

"Right across the street from you. We bought the whole block. In fact, the scaffolding just went up."

"I noticed. But I have a question."

"Shoot."

"Why does the city need this building?"

"Do you know how much of the Twin Towers was leased by the city, state, and federal government?"

"A shitload?" Steeg said.

"More than that. I can have Riverview up and running in a year, and I have the contacts to start filling the place."

"Lucky you."

"But there's a problem."

"Me, pissing in the punch."

"Bingo! We haven't got all our ducks in a row with variances and air rights and building codes." Sloan paused to adjust his French cuffs. "It's a very touchy situation, as I'm sure you can appreciate."

Not to mention screwing up the view from my apartment, Steeg thought.

"Certainly."

"Then you come along with your bullshit investigation of a dead hooker instead of leaving it to the police."

"Murdered, actually."

"Whatever. Anyway, some things are gonna come out, things that are better left unsaid."

"Like Gideon El boffing Diana Strickland?"

Sloan's forehead popped with tiny beads of sweat. "Well, yes."

"And Gideon El is a partner in this enterprise, so the press is gonna have a field day."

Sloan looked at Mallus and Gideon El. "I told you he was smart." He turned back to Steeg. "Yeah, Gideon did have a dalliance with her, but that's all it was. He didn't kill her. Moore did."

"And who killed Moore?"

"Who the fuck knows? Maybe it was your Indian."

"He does get around. Maybe he did cock robin too."

"For God's sake, Gideon El has a family — are you gonna ruin it for them too?"

"Perhaps."

Gideon El looked like he was about to be sick.

"There's always room for another partner, Jake. This could mean a lot of money to you."

"Are you attempting to bribe me?"

"Are you wearing a wire?"

"No.

With a nod of his head, Sloan gestured to Mallus to check.

"If he lays one hand on me, he'll be eating salads through a straw."

Mallus backed off.

"Let's call it a business opportunity for a friend. So, what do you say?"

"Sounds great, but think of all the money you'd save if the Indian manages to get lucky."

CHAPTER TWENTY-SEVEN

Steeg was on the way home when his cell phone rang. He flipped the lid and put it to his ear.

"I miss you," Caroline said.

"I love it when you talk dirty."

"I'm serious. Can you come over?"

"Sure. You're my first call on my new phone. How did you get my number?"

"DeeDee gave it to me. We had a long talk. She's very nice."

"You too."

"When can I expect you?"

"What are you wearing?"

"A sad smile," Caroline said.

"I'm on my way."

"Take a cab."

"If I keep breaking my rules, I'll lose the inner me."

"That wouldn't be so terrible," she said, hanging up.

Steeg walked toward Ninth Avenue and spotted the Indian checking out the window of Your Heart's Desire, a porn shop on Forty-seventh Street. He walked up to him.

"Hi," Steeg said.

The Indian turned around, not at all surprised.

"Looka here, it's you again. Seems the Lord has put you on my trail once again."

"Or vice versa."

"He works in strange and mysterious ways."

Steeg gestured at the window. "Checking out the merchandise?"

He smiled. "And the Lord unleashed his terrible wrath on Sodom and Gomorrah."

"Do you have a name?"

"That's mighty kind of you to ask. Name's Floyd. Samael Floyd. And you, sir?"

"You know my name."

The Indian shrugged. "Guess we're not gonna be friends."

"Why'd you do a war dance in my apartment, Samael?"

"Are you mocking me, sir?"

"You might say."

"I don't take kindly to that."

"I don't give a shit."

A muscle in the hinge of the Indian's jaw vibrated like a tuning fork. "I don't tolerate profanity."

"If I see you again, I'm gonna put one in your wheel-house. Understand?"

"You tellin' me you marked the boundaries of this big ol' city with your scent and I got to stay out?"

"Something like that," Steeg said.

The Indian smiled, but his eyes were flat. "Go in peace, pilgrim."

***

Caroline Strickland's East Sixty-third Street apartment overlooked the East River and Roosevelt Island. To the north was Hell Gate, a once-treacherous, roiling stretch of water that in Revolutionary times swallowed a British pay ship, a three-master, believed to be carrying hundreds of millions of dollars' worth of gold bullion. The bullion still lay in the river's bed, guarded by the currents and whirlpools that had claimed it. To the south was the Brooklyn Bridge, its cables strung like the strings of a great harp.

Her apartment was as different from her father's as the Metropolitan Museum of Art was from MoMA, all white and black and sharp-edged; a space filled with smooth lines and contrasts. Much like Caroline.

She was true to her word. She greeted him at the door wearing only a sad smile.

"Since you're becoming a regular here, would you like a tour of the apartment?" she said.

"Where does it start?"

"The bedroom."

Afterward, they lay together on a tangle of sheets with their hips barely touching. "Your hospitality is overwhelming," Steeg said.

Caroline smiled and nestled closer, slinging a leg over his thigh. "And you haven't even seen the den yet."

She smelled of lilac and talcum powder.

"Is it different?"

"Better," she said, snuggling closer.

He made little ringlets of her hair with his fingers. "Not possible."

She slid her hand under the sheet and stroked him. "You'll see."

"What's it like growing up rich?"

"The same as growing up poor, only there's more money," Caroline said.

"That's a non sequitur."

"No, that's me being endearing."

It was dark, and the lighted trams looked like giant fireflies floating over the river between Roosevelt Island and Manhattan.

"You're not a bit like your father," Steeg said.

"Few people are."

"I had a talk with John Sayres."

"Sweet man."

"He said that after your mother's death, your father treated you much better than Diana."

"I was the good child."

"I don't think it was as simple as that."

She disengaged and sat up, wrapping the sheet around her. "Are we getting serious now?"

"There's just so much I don't know, too many unconnected dots."

"Like?"

"Why did he single out Diana for his special brand of affection?"

"What are you implying?"

"He sexually abused her."

"You're kidding."

"Unfortunately, no."

"How can you say such a thing?"

"I'm not, Sayres is. Claims that the nannies knew

but were too afraid of your father to blow the whistle."

"I don't believe it! He's a bastard, not a molester."

"Sayres has no reason to lie. He's dying. Pancreatic cancer."

Caroline's eyes watered. "I . . . I didn't know."

"Dr. Weldon agrees with him."

"Her psychiatrist? Why didn't she report him?"

"She's in your father's pocket."

She ran her fingers back and forth through her hair. "I had no idea. You have to remember, I was a child myself. When I was eight I was packed off to boarding school. How would I possibly know what he was up to?"

"But you admit the possibility?"

She looked away. "With my father, anything is possible."

"Fair enough. But later on, when you two were older, did Diana mention anything about it?"

"No, never. We were never close. Never shared the intimate details of our lives. No girl talk. I guess we were both private people." She paused. "It explains a lot. The drugs, the promiscuity, the downward spiral. That son of a bitch!"

"Too bad we can't pick our parents ahead of time."

Caroline said nothing.

"You mentioned that Diana witnessed your mother's death." He paused. "And she changed right afterward."

Caroline nodded. "She told me years later. Diana was in therapy at the time. She was always in therapy. Anyway, she claimed she saw a man enter the apartment, attack Mother, and throw her off the terrace."

"Did you believe her?"

"Up to now, no. She was a baby, how could she possibly remember that? I thought it was 'recovered memory' psychobabble. On top of that, Diana was an addict. Would you have believed her?"

"No, but you threw her 'recovered memory' in your father's face. If you didn't believe it, why use it?"

She turned away. "I wonder about that myself."

"So, there may be something to it?"

"I —"

The muffled ring of a cell phone cut Caroline off. "It's not mine," she said.

"How do you know?"

"Mine plays George Jones's 'He Stopped Lovin' Her Today.' "

Steeg was in love.

"Damn it!" he said, reaching to the floor for his pants. "I knew this would happen." He flipped the lid open. "This is not a good time!"

"Like I give a shit!" Luce said. "You better get home right now."

CHAPTER TWENTY-EIGHT

When Steeg arrived home, Luce and Cherise were there; they had the dazed, grim-eyed look of people waiting for something terrible to happen, something outside of their power to change. The television was turned up loud. On the screen, a weather lady with puffy hair and a bouncy smile pointed to the jet stream undulating across the continent like a giant earthworm. Luce sat staring into space at the kitchen table, drumming a monotonous riff on the Formica with her three-inch purple-and-green-colored fingernails. Cherise sat on the edge of an easy chair, unable to take her eyes off DeeDee, whose arms were tightly lashed around her knees. DeeDee's eyes were wet, and her face was the color of spoiled milk. Steeg sat down beside her and gently wrapped her in his arms, a gesture intended to be both protective and reassuring but accomplishing neither. His fingers lightly swept back loose strands of hair matted on her forehead. She mumbled something he didn't understand and burrowed her face in his chest.

He turned to Luce. "What happened?"

"We figured we'd take DeeDee out to dinner.

Knowin' your deal with ethnic restaurants, we took her to Tang Fong's, on Fiftieth. Szechuan."

Steeg knew what was coming.

"Your Indian shows up," she said.

"In the restaurant?"

"No, he's waiting for us when we come out. Biggest son of a bitch I ever saw. Like a garbage truck with arms."

"One very scary man," Cherise agreed, working a cigarette down to the filter. "Had his hair done up in these long, black braids. Eyes the same color, looked like the bottom of an inkpot. No whites at all."

"My guy wears a ponytail."

"Yeah? Well, he went to the hairdresser," Luce said.

"Did he lay his hands on you?"

"Didn't have to. The weird look on his face was enough to scare the hell out of me, and I was armed."

DeeDee stirred, and Steeg loosened his embrace.

"He had this Bible in his hand," Cherise said. "Knew our names. Said he was Samael Floyd. Asked if we enjoyed the meal." A shudder rippled through her body. "If a snake could talk, he would sound like him. Asked if he could pray with us, smiling this psycho smile like he knew things about us we wouldn't even admit to ourselves."

"And?"

"I took a look at DeeDee and was afraid she was gonna pee herself," Luce said. "I told him to get lost."

Cherise broke in. "He was very polite. Kept talkin' about how we've got to be saved, baptized in the Blood, or we'll be damned to eternal perdition."

The snakes in Steeg's head began to uncoil.

"Sounds like Samael."

"That's when I pulled my piece and jammed it under his eye," Luce said.

"It didn't matter, did it?"

"Uh-uh. Just stood there amused with the whole thing. This evil, sour smell was just flowin' off him in waves. I felt like my skin was crawlin' with ants."

"What did he do?"

"Nothin', and that's what really got to me. It gave me the creeps, like rats runnin' over my grave."

DeeDee broke Steeg's embrace and inched away. She rewrapped her arms around her knees and rocked to and fro with the precision of a metronome.

"Then he turns to DeeDee, tells her how pretty she is, how it's too bad her mama's not around to help her through the sad times. And that's when the balloon goes up. She gets hysterical and takes off runnin'. Cherise went after her, and I guess I got distracted, but it was no more than a second or two. When I turned, he was gone. Just disappeared into the air like some kind of wraith. Damnedest thing I ever saw."

CHAPTER TWENTY-NINE

Most people hit the cosmic lottery and live out their lives blissfully unaware that a man like Samael Floyd exists. They spend their days dipping more or less equally from the barrels of good times and hard, never dreaming that someone shining with his unique brand of incandescent madness could show up at their door. The others, those few whose orbits intersect with his by happenstance or cruel design, find themselves seriously questioning the existence of a loving God. Steeg refused to wait. He tucked the Beretta into his waistband and went looking for him.

He knew he wouldn't find him. Floyd was one of those creatures that lived in cracks in the earth where polarity was reversed and the laws of nature suspended. He inhabited a negative universe where acts of goodness and compassion and love were blasphemies.

Trying to draw Floyd out of his hidey-hole wasn't going to be easy. The only way was to paint a target on his back and walk the streets of Hell's Kitchen.

Gritty moonlight bathed the streets with a dull patina.

Walking south, Steeg passed through the Meatpacking District, where herds of goggle-eyed cattle lowing with fear had once walked the same streets on their way to the slaughterhouse. Now, clusters of transvestites beckoned to him from the same shadows. He walked north past the piers, wearing his anger like a tight-fitting caul, and then up and down the side streets, sensing Floyd's presence, feeling his eyes lasing holes in his back. But Floyd wasn't playing. After two hours he gave it up, knowing that he would never find him. It was Floyd's play. He would pick the time and place of their next meeting.

Luce was awake when he returned home.

"Everything calmed down?" Steeg said.

"Cherise and DeeDee are finally asleep, but calmed down? It's gonna be a while before that happens."

"How come you're still up?"

"Made some phone calls to a buddy pullin' the twelve-to-eight. Had him go into the FBI's Violent Criminal Apprehension Program database and find out about our friend the Indian. Want some coffee? Made a fresh pot."

"No. What did he have to say?"

"Floyd's one piece of work. Originally from North Carolina. Enlisted in the army, joined the Rangers. Distinguished Service Cross, Bronze Star, a dyed-in-the-wool hero. But, get this: He blows up his career and gets booted out with an Undesirable Discharge."

"The only way that happens is if he screws his C.O.'s wife."

"His records are sealed, so it's anyone's guess. Anyway, it was a watershed moment. It was all downhill after that. Didn't adjust well to civilian life. Pretty soon he starts buildin' a record. Aggravated assault, battery, all physical stuff. No drugs, no sexual offenses, no theft. Just likes to beat up on people. Never served a day. Vics and witnesses were too frightened to testify. About twelve years ago he did a really bad assault. They had to put the vic, a Mississippi cop, in witness protection to get him to testify. The Indian did a jolt at Parchman. When he got out, he found the cop. Did him and his family. No witnesses."

"Our friend is a charmer."

"You don't know the half of it. A couple of months later, he kills a cop in Louisiana."

"Seems to have authority issues."

"You might say. They put him in Angola, the second stop on his grand tour of the prison system. It should have been his last. I'm from there, and I know. The only way you leave Angola is in a pine box."

"But not our friend."

"Right, not the Indian. Somehow he escapes. How in hell he made it through those swamps is a wonder. Been at large for eight years."

"Clearly, he didn't retire," Steeg said.

"Uh-uh. Police all over the country are trying to clear their cold cases by puttin' unsolved murders and disappearances on him. Trouble is, he has no M.O., no trademark way of killin'."

"I can't wait to hear about his softer, gentler side," Steeg said.

"Don't get your hopes up," Luce said. "He was pretty much isolated while in prison. Ain't too many Indians enjoying the hospitality of the state in Parchman or Angola. He wasn't a brother, so he couldn't look to the Crips and Bloods for protection. The Aryan Brotherhood wouldn't take him, and neither would the Hispanic gangs. That meant he was fair game. Everybody's punchboard. After a week, guys like him usually wind up wearin' a bra and panties and turned out in the Yard and sold for a pack of cigarettes a throw."

"But not our Indian?"

"The minute he cleared processin' and hit the Yard, they all came at him, stone killers and men with fish guts for brains. He was the last man standin'. Got to the point they were all scared shitless of him. They figured if they couldn't beat him, might as well use him. He became an equal-opportunity enforcer for anyone with the money to pay him."

"And that's why he wears the teardrop tattoos under his eye."

"And he earned every one of them," Luce said. "By the way, you know what they called him?"

"I'll bet it wasn't Chief."

"Death."

"Catchy."

"That ain't the least of it."

"I can hardly wait."

"His name struck me as odd — not Samuel, but Samael. I Googled it. Turns out it's a another name for Satan."

"His parents must have had one hell of a sense of humor."

"Or, they were foot-washin' Baptists a couple of bolts short of a gross."

"Or," Steeg said, "they knew what they had on their hands."

CHAPTER THIRTY

It was almost dawn, and Luce had finally gone to bed. Steeg, with the sour taste of copper pennies in his mouth, went up to the roof. It was Saturday morning, and the city was unnaturally quiet. A brackish breeze blew in from the Hudson. He leaned against a wall, closed his eyes, and waited for the butterflies.

It's the time when Irish warriors ride the skies.

Norah Dowd Steeg stands on the roof with her young boys, waiting for the first glimmerings of the sun's reddish-orange glow to rise from the netherworld. At the precise moment when the horizon turns a pale pink, she points to the clouds, now visible on the horizon.

"There they are, do you see them?" she says, her voice musical with the cadences of thick sod, dewy mornings, and days filled with promise. "Look, they're astride their great stallions."

Dave and Jackson look up at the purple-bottomed clouds ringed with fire.

"There's Finn McCool and Mahon with their faces painted blue," she says, pointing out their features in the rounded edges and hues of the clouds. "And fair

Cu Chulainn wielding his terrible ax. Aye, aren't they beautiful."

Each warrior has his own story, a tale of epic battles, lost love, and searing tragedy. But her heart belongs to Brian Boru, and so does Dave's.

"And look there, boys, over the Empire State Building, The High King of Tara, Brian Boru comes."

Her trove of Brian Boru tales is inexhaustible, but Dave's favorite is the one about the butterflies.

After all the storytelling is done, Norah announces that it's time for breakfast.

Dave refuses to budge. "Didn't you forget something, Ma?"

She looks puzzled. "Sure I don't think so, Davey."

It's a game they play.

"About Brian and Ivar?"

Her face brightens with recognition. "Oh, that one. Of course. How could I forget?"

Dave smiles.

She cups his face in her hands.

"This is a truly great story, so you have to pay attention. Vikings had invaded the land, destroying churches, burning crops, and killing everyone who crossed their heathen paths. Their leader, King Ivar, was a giant of a man with flame for a beard and calluses like oak bark on his hands. Oh, a brute, he was, and ugly to boot."

Her sons stare at her, fascinated.

"Now Brian was the handsomest and bravest man in all of Ireland, but when they met on the field of battle, he saw that his force was half the size of the heathen Ivar. Aye, it was going to be a terrible day for the Irish. But *then Brian had a grand idea. He challenged Ivar the Ugly to single combat on the following morning, and the Viking foolishly agreed."*

"But there was a problem," Dave says.

"Aye, a big problem. The Viking camp lay on the western side of the field, and that meant that the morning sun would be in Brian's eyes. What to do?"

"He prayed," Dave says."

Her broad face crinkles into a smile. "You're a smart boy, Davey. He prayed for a miracle. And while he slept, the butterflies came out of the forest, millions and billions of them, and flew up to the sun. And with the beating of their wings moved the sun across the sky to the west."

Dave leaps to his feet.

"And when Brian woke up, the sun was in Ivar's eyes, and Brian cut his ugly head off and stuck it on the point of his sword and jabbed it at the Vikings. And they ran from Ireland never to return."

Norah sweeps him into her arms. Dave is beaming. "It was a happy ending, Davey."

"I like happy endings."

Steeg opened his eyes and looked up. The sky was cobalt blue and cloudless. Morning sunlight painted the streets yellow. He found it unalterably depressing. He pulled out his cell phone and punched in Dave's number.

CHAPTER THIRTY-ONE

Steeg met Dave at the Westway Diner, on Forty-forth Street. The letter "E" had been missing from the sign set on the roof for as long as he could remember. The diner was packed with construction workers, and white-uniformed sailors off a recently arrived cruise ship. In some strange tacit agreement, the sailors sat at the counter and the construction workers occupied the booths. Dave, who had arrived first, sat in a booth in the back, and Steeg slid in opposite him.

"I ordered breakfast for you," Dave said. "Eggs over hard, hash browns, and sausage patties, not links. Well done. Just the way you like them."

Dave wore a banker's pinstripe gray suit. A napkin tucked in at his neck protected the front of his starched white shirt and solid red tie.

"I'm impressed. You remembered I hate runny eggs," Steeg said.

"You used to say it was like eating mucous," Dave smiled at the memory. "But you're right: I never forget anything, not an insult or a kindness. Besides, how many brothers do I have?"

Their food came, and Steeg picked at it.

Dave eyed him. "Something wrong?"

Steeg dropped the fork on his plate. "It's not the food."

"Then what is it?"

Steeg told Dave about Samael Floyd.

Dave's face darkened. "Why didn't you come to me sooner?"

Steeg was about to cross a line that they had tacitly agreed was not a subject for discussion. "We don't talk business, remember?"

"This isn't business, it's you."

"That's why I'm here."

Dave plucked at an earlobe. "There's something I don't figure. If he's coming at you, why hasn't he made his move yet?"

"Maybe in his psycho mind he's softening me up. Toying with me like it's some kind of weird foreplay. Who knows what crazy people think and why they do what they do?"

Dave's fingers strayed to his cheek, stroking its pebbled texture with infinite softness. "He's a fuckin' dead man."

Steeg shifted nervously in his seat. "I don't think so. It's like catching smoke with a net."

"Bullshit, he's a man."

"I can handle him," Steeg said, without much conviction.

"Yeah, like you have up to now. Please spare me the crap." He paused. "Any ideas who he's working for?"

"No. I went through the usual suspects, Gideon El, Mallus, Terry, but it just doesn't add up. Terry told me about his new project to make a buck out of 9/11, and that's more his style. Told me I was getting in the way. But hire a guy like this nightmare? It's hard to believe."

"I agree. Guys like them have no compunctions about stealing the coins off a dead man's eyes. But murder? Uh-uh." Dave took a sip of his coffee. "Okay, what do you want me to do?"

"Take DeeDee until everything settles down. The Indian knows where I'm vulnerable, and I don't want him hurting her. She'll be safe with you, and Luce and Cherise can get back to their own lives."

"Consider it done. We're leaving today to visit Anthony at Dartmouth. Should be back late tomorrow afternoon. I'll call when I get in."

"I appreciate it, Dave."

"My pleasure. In the meantime, I'll try to get a line on your Indian. Okay?"

"Thanks."

"All right. Now that that's off your mind, have some breakfast. It's getting cold.

Steeg dotted the patty with maple syrup and cut it into quarters. He popped a piece in his mouth. "It's good. God, I love diners. They have menus as thick as a phonebook — you could have everything from Italian to matzoh ball soup. How can you beat it?"

Dave signaled the waitress for fresh coffee. "It's the best. So, what else is going on?"

"Dominic stopped by the other day," Steeg said.

"Talk about your nightmares. What did he want?"

"Wondering how things were going on the Strickland investigation. He doesn't look good."

"Neither did I when he got finished with me."

"I know, but I was thinking of the butterflies this morning."

Dave laughed. "And the epic battle between the Brian and Ivar the Ugly? God, I miss her. Franny's the closest I'm ever gonna get to Mom. Never cheated on Franny. Never will."

"That's exactly my point. You're not a bargain, either, but Franny saw something in you."

"Is there a point in there?"

"Maybe Norah saw something in Dominic that we missed. She loved him enough to marry him. That's got to count for something."

"So?"

"So, how about we put the baggage behind us and take him out to dinner one night. I mean, you're the one who keeps talking about family. Don't you think it's time we started behaving like one? He doesn't even know your kids."

Dave ripped the napkin off and threw it on the table. "I'll call you tomorrow."

CHAPTER THIRTY-TWO

DeeDee woke up at eight in the morning, overcome with claustrophobia. Living with her father, a man who shouldn't have been allowed to raise tomatoes, much less a child, was bad enough, but four people crammed into a small one-bedroom apartment was becoming intolerable. With Floyd on the loose, Steeg had kept her home from school, which translated to no friends and no break from three pairs of watchful eyes. DeeDee was at the point where Steeg's nutty idea about tae kwon do was starting to look good. The apartment had the smoky aroma of sizzling bacon and fresh-brewed coffee. She threw on jeans and one of Steeg's NYPD sweatshirts and padded into the kitchen. Luce, wearing a saffron yellow terry cloth robe, was at the stove dipping thick wedges of bread into an egg batter.

"How're you doin', kid?" she said. "Sleep well?"

"Okay," DeeDee lied. "Where's Steeg?"

Luce plucked the bacon from the pan, laid it on a paper towel, and set the battered bread in the hot bacon grease.

"Out and about. Want some breakfast? Makin' some biscuits, too, in case you don't like French toast."

DeeDee speared a bacon strip and bit off the end. "I'm not hungry."

"I can see that. Want to sit with me while I eat?"

She looked out of the window. "Uh-uh. I think I'm going downstairs for a while. Sit on the stoop, get some air."

"Give me fifteen minutes and I'll keep you company."

"I'd rather be alone."

"You think that's a good idea after last night?"

DeeDee exploded. "I feel like I'm in lockdown and you're my keeper. Can't I have *some* privacy?"

Luce remembered how things were back when she was DeeDee's age. Adolescent hormones kicked in, and everyone who even remotely resembled an adult was the enemy. And when you added DeeDee's upside-down life to the mix, you had combustion. Luce wanted to cut her some slack, but Cherise was at work and the Indian was still out there somewhere.

"I respect that, but just so far. You're goin' through things no child deserves, and you're feelin' sorry for yourself, and that's normal. But you've got to believe that it's temporary. Things are goin' to be lookin' up sooner than later."

DeeDee exploded. "I hate you, and I hate Steeg, and I hate living like this! I don't have any life, at all."

"I ain't too fond of it myself. But that's the way it is."

"Please, Luce?"

"I said no."

DeeDee sidled up to her, wrapped her arms around her, and snuggled in. "Pretty please? I promise I won't go off the stoop. I just need to get out for a few minutes. Be alone."

Luce was tired of arguing. She checked her watch. Against her better judgment, she decided to cut her a little bit of slack. "I'll make a deal with you. I'm gonna take a shower, so you've got a half an hour. And don't be wanderin' off, I'll be lookin' out the window."

"Thank you, thank you, thank you," DeeDee said, heading out the door.

When she reached the street, she sat down on the steps, squeezed her temples between her fists, and began to cry.

"'Sup, little sister?" The voice was crooning and seductive.

She looked up, and saw Dman looming above her. The hood was down on his black sweat suit, and his dreadlocks hung down to his shoulders. A large gold medallion hung from a linked gold chain around his neck. Her gaze strayed to the tops of her sneakers.

"Go away!"

He sat down next to her, sprawling on the steps, making a big show of getting comfortable. "Why you do me that way, girl? Just tryin' to be friendly, and you ain't given me no props."

DeeDee knew Dman's reputation and that Steeg didn't like him, but his attention made her feel warm inside. She edged away, but not too far, nervously looking up to see if Luce was watching. She dried her eyes on her sleeve, unsure of what to say.

He reached into a pocket and pulled out a green

plastic cigarette lighter and a blunt as big around as a sausage.

"You better not be doin' that," she said. "There are cops right upstairs."

He smiled and lit the tip of the blunt and brought it to his lips.

"Dman is right with Five-Oh. No problems." Closing his eyes, he inhaled deeply, then slowly expelled the smoke in a thin stream.

He held the blunt out to her, as if it were the most natural thing in the world. DeeDee knew that Luce was right, she *was* feeling sorry for herself. Her life was out of her control. She lived in a strange house with three cops babysitting her every move. *Why not?* she thought.

Dman inched over until their thighs touched. "Ain't gonna bite ya," he coaxed, bringing it to her lips.

"That's not such a good idea, friend." The voice was deep, carrying a hint of menace.

Floyd had materialized out of nowhere. His braids were combed out, and his hair hung like a lustrous black mantilla down the middle of his back.

DeeDee's arms wrapped themselves around her thin frame so tight that her fingertips touched at her back. Her mouth formed a perfect oval. No sound came out, but the voice in her brain screamed for Luce.

Dman looked up through yellowish, red-tinged eyes. "Who the fuck are you?"

"Doesn't really matter now, does it? I think you'd best be movin' on."

"Yo, ain't got no horse, Tonto. Maybe I can borrow

yours," he said, gripped in a paroxysm of giggling.

"Be careful what you wish for, pilgrim."

"Fuck you talkin' about?" Dman said, switching the blunt to his left hand and bringing it to his lips. The tip glowed red as he pulled on it.

Floyd stared at Dman. The muscles in his face tightened, and his voice was very soft.

"And I looked, and beheld a pale horse, and his name that sat on him was Death." Floyd's eyes were pure black stones. "And Hell followed with him." His voice rose. "And power was given unto them over the fourth part of the earth."

In a lazy, barely noticeable motion, Dman slipped his right hand into the pocket of his sweatsuit.

Floyd's voice seemed to billow from a dark place deep inside. "To kill with sword, and with hunger."

Dman's fingers tightened around the rough grip of a .22 caliber revolver.

"And with *death!*"

Floyd took a step back and kicked Dman in the face, smashing his nose with a sickening crunch. Blood spattered like strings of rubies.

DeeDee's arms tightened their grip as a feeling worse than fear rippled through her body.

"And," Floyd said, wrapping Dman's dreadlocks in his fists and flinging him into the street as if he were a rag doll, "he opened the bottomless pit, and unto the scorpions was given power."

Like a great cat, Floyd pounced on him, his fists rising and falling like pistons, his fingers tearing large hanks of hair from Dman's head, leaving his scalp bloody.

The carnage continued for several minutes before he pulled Dman to his feet. He put his face very close to his and spoke in a low voice.

"You are a corrupter of the innocent and a despoiler of orphans. Eye for an eye, measure for measure."

Dman wasn't in any condition to argue.

Floyd released his grip, and Dman slumped to the ground. Floyd turned to DeeDee, his face and hair painted red with Dman's blood.

"I'm sorry you ain't got your momma with you. A girl needs her momma. She'd a tole you to have no truck with trash like that." He paused. "One other thing. Tell Steeg that he's in over his head and if he doesn't pull back, I'll be comin' for him."

CHAPTER THIRTY-THREE

Late Sunday afternoon, Dave and Franny picked up DeeDee. It was one of those days that weather forecasters called "a false spring," a cheating illusion that better days were on the way. The temperature reached a balmy seventy-two degrees, people in shirtsleeves were on the streets, and, like a flock of great seabirds, sailboats appeared on the Hudson. Floyd had left DeeDee an emotional wreck and put Dman on the critical list at Bellevue. Although both would ultimately heal, Steeg knew that it would take DeeDee longer.

Luce and Cherise flanked her, holding her arms as she sleepwalked to Dave's BMW sedan. Steeg followed with her suitcase. Dave held the door open while Franny helped her into the backseat. She slipped in bedside DeeDee and gently drew her head to her lap. Dave closed the door and took DeeDee's suitcase from Steeg.

"She gonna be all right?"

"I hope so," Steeg replied. "Kids are resilient."

"Yeah," Dave said. "Just look at us." He walked around to the back and placed the suitcase in the trunk. Steeg followed him.

"I haven't heard anything about your psycho Indian," Dave said. "But I've got a feeling he won't be bothering you anymore."

"So, you know who sent him."

"I didn't say that. I put the word out that I would pay big if someone delivered me his scalp. It'll get some attention." He looked at DeeDee through the rear window. "Poor kid. Franny will take good care of her. At least that's one thing you don't have to worry about."

"I appreciate it."

"I know that you're goin' to say no, but you're welcome to stay too, y'know."

"I'll think about it."

Dave pulled a face. "Sure, you will. Anyway, it's a standing offer."

"You better go."

Dave slammed the lid shut. "Yeah, I'll be in touch." He walked around to the driver's side and opened the door. "One other thing. Set the dinner up with Dominic."

Steeg was surprised. "Why the change of heart?"

"Franny," Dave said. "You know how she is about family. Anyway, make the arrangements and I'll be there." He closed the door, started up the engine, and drove off.

Steeg turned to Luce and Cherise. "It's been a little slice of heaven while it lasted, but now it's your turn to say good-bye."

"Are you nuts?" Luce said. "Floyd told DeeDee that he still intends to settle up with you. Frankly, I don't want to see you endin' up at Bellevue as Dman's roommate, or in the basement lyin' on a gurney in the morgue."

"Neither do I."

"So, we're stayin'."

"No, you're going. Dave has my back. Floyd won't get within fifty yards of me before someone pops him." Steeg didn't believe a word of it, but he didn't want them hurt. "I just don't want you and Cherise as collateral damage."

Cherise broke in. "As much as I hate to admit it, Steeg's right, Luce. We were supposed to protect DeeDee and so far we've been a bust. It's like Floyd is one of those Vietcong tunnel rats popping up out of nowhere, scaring the shit out of us and disappearing the same way he came."

Luce gave a grudging shrug. "But we just can't walk away."

"I don't see how we're helpin'," Cherise said.

"Don't you hate when you're part of a conversation and people speak of you in the third person?" Steeg said. "Look, I'm with Cherise on this one. The best way you can help me is by following police procedures. Floyd committed an assault on Dman. If I remember correctly, that's a crime. And DeeDee will testify to that. So will Dman, if he ever wakes up. Report it. This way, I'll not only have Dave's guys, but forty thousand cops watching my back. How can I lose?"

"I'd say you're in deep shit," Luce said.

CHAPTER THIRTY-FOUR

Three days had passed, and Floyd had yet to make an appearance anywhere but in Steeg's head. With all the other stuff going on in there, it was getting to be a very busy place. Life, Steeg realized, was a lot simpler when he was a drunk. To bring some order to the chaos, he decided to focus his energies on the thing he did best, finding the bad guys, and that took him back to the beginning and to Dman.

Originally a combination almshouse, penitentiary, and quarantine site for victims of the 1794 yellow fever plague, the twenty-five-story Bellevue Hospital overlooked a shabby stretch of the East River. Courtesy of Samael Floyd and pending gun and possession charges, it was Dman's home until his arraignment.

The false spring of the weekend had given way to a day that was a raw wound. The temperature had dropped back into the low thirties, and an icy rain was falling.

Dman's room was painted a tubercular white and smelled strongly of disinfectant. A grimy, barred window barely let in what little light there was. Those parts of Dman's head and face that weren't swathed in bandages were a mass of reddish-purple knots, lumps, and bruises. His right wrist was shackled to the bed frame. He saw Steeg, and his eyes widened with a mixture of shock and fear.

"Don't bother to get up," Steeg said.

He took Dman's metal-jacketed chart from the foot of the bed frame, flipped it open, and pulled a chair up to the side of the bed.

Dman's eyes warily followed him.

"According to this, the Indian dropped you into a Cuisinart. Most of the bones in your face are splintered, three fractured ribs, collapsed lung, fractured skull, and plastic surgery to repair your scalp." Steeg grinned a devilish grin. "I guess a career in modeling is out."

He snapped the chart closed, making a noise like a gunshot.

The sound made Dman jump.

"I hate to say I told you so, but you should have listened to me and stayed away from DeeDee. Seems she has the unlikeliest of people looking out for her, like a crazed Indian."

"What . . . the fuck . . . *you* . . . want?" Dman croaked.

"Funny you should ask. I have some time on my hands lately and I've been doing some thinking, something I strongly recommend you take up once what's left of your brains unscramble. Anyway, since you're the neighborhood candy man, I figure that you've got an interesting customer list."

Dman stared at a spider spinning a web in a corner where the ceiling and the walls met.

Steeg continued. "How about I mention some names."

Apparently, Dman found the spider's activity endlessly fascinating. He didn't respond.

"Does Graham Moore ring a bell?"

Dman remained stone-faced.

"How about Diana Strickland?"

Same response.

Steeg picked up a box of tissues from the night table and leaned over and whacked him on the bridge of his nose just hard enough to get his attention.

"Oh, shit!" Dman screamed, bolting into a sitting position while trying unsuccessfully to bring his manacled hand to his face. His eyes watered and tears streamed down. "What the fuck you do that for?"

"You didn't appear to be listening. And, by the way, next time I smack your nose, use your left hand, moron."

"Fuck next time. Where's the cop supposed to be outside?"

"Taking a leak." Steeg raised the box again. "Listen, you abscess, the party's just starting unless we have some honesty here."

"I don't know what the fuck you're talking about," he said, gingerly touching his nose with the fingers of his left hand.

"No pain, no gain," Steeg said, drawing back the box for an encore performance.

"Hold on! Wait a minute! What's in it for me?"

Steeg lowered the box to his lap and leaned in. "Somehow, I thought you'd see it my way. You've had quite a busy career, Rahim. Even putting your juvie record aside, you're staring down the barrel of two felonies, gun possession and possession with intent to sell. Along with a prior for armed robbery, I make that three strikes and you're out. They're gonna love you at Sing Sing."

"Bullshit! My lawyer'll plead that down to Class B misdemeanors. It's a skate, my man. A walk in the park."

"That's really clear thinking, Clarence Darrow. When I get through telling the prosecutor all about how you pushed a blunt on a sweet little thirteen-year-old girl, do you honestly think your Legal Aid schmuck right out of law school is gonna stand a chance? By the end of my testimony, you're gonna be sliced and diced and on the bus."

Dman's face creased into a pained expression. "Why're you doin' this to me? I do what I gotta do to live, man."

"Spare me the 'up from poverty' crap. I'm not your social worker, so I don't give a shit about how hard a life you had or what made you turn into a piece of garbage. See, you made a big mistake when you screwed with DeeDee. I warned you, but apparently it wasn't strong enough. My mistake. Think of me as that spider up on the wall. You're mine now, Rahim, and there ain't no way around it. So what's it gonna be?"

Dman turned to Steeg. "I get to plead to two misdemeanors, no jail time."

Steeg got to his feet. "Good-bye, Rahim. Enjoy the rest of your incarcerated life."

"Okay, it was Moore. I sold to him."

"Not Strickland?"

"Uh-uh, just Moore."

"How many times is your junk stepped on before it gets to you?"

"Five, six times, who the fuck knows? It's runnin' about fifteen to twenty percent pure."

"Why'd you sell him a hot shot?"

"I ain't goin' down for that, okay? I need your word."

"Fine, just answer the question."

"A white guy shows up one day, shaved head, fuckin' studs up and down his ears. Never saw him before. Slips me a packet marked 'Sweet Dreams,' or some shit like that. Tells me the next time Moore makes a buy to give it to him. An hour later, Moore shows up. That's all I know."

"When was this?"

"The night they found the ho in his room."

"Who sent him?"

"Fuck if I know."

"So, let me get this straight. A perfect stranger shows up out of the blue and tells you to sell a specific packet of shit to Moore, and you do it because you're an accommodating sort?" Steeg headed for the door. "Deal's off, asshole!"

"Wait! It's the troof. He showed up with my distributor, a Dominican dude named Soto."

"And where can I find this Soto?"

"Wildwood Cemetery, on Long Island."

Caroline was feeling light-headed. She had just returned home from a mainly liquid lunch with friends and was paying for it. Her mouth was dry, and the skin on her face felt tight. She threw her coat over the back of the nearest chair and walked into the kitchen. She opened the refrigerator, retrieved a bottle of water, and headed for the living room. When she reached the sofa, she sat down, unscrewed the cap, and tipped the bottle to her lips, draining half of it. She reached over and placed the bottle on the coffee table. She kicked off her shoes, swung her body around, and stretched out on the cushions. Within seconds, her eyes were closed.

"Shhh."

The sound was faraway and barely audible.

Caroline stirred, and adjusted the throw pillow beneath her head.

"Shhh."

The sound was closer, like the rustling of a rattler's tail.

Caroline's eyes fluttered open.

Floyd was bent over her, his finger pressed to his lips. A large, oval piece of polished turquoise swung hypnotically from a leather cord strung around his neck.

Her eyes registered him, but her brain lagged a beat behind.

In those few milliseconds he bent lower, so close that the sheets of his hair framed both of their faces. She saw her reflection in the black mirrors of his eyes. In that moment of twisted intimacy he became her entire world, and the madness shining in his face was the only illumination.

She smelled him now, a raw, loamy odor, like rotting vegetation. A suffocating warmth traveled up from her groin until it colored her face. She struggled for breath.

He brought his finger to her cheek and lightly traced the line of her jaw. "Shhh," he repeated. "No need to hurt you," he whispered. "If you do what I say." His finger moved to her cheek. "Now you just nod if you understand."

Her head moved in assent.

"I know all about you," he whispered. "Know what you're thinkin', know what you're feelin'."

His finger moved down her throat to the swell of her breast, where its tip lightly circled her nipple.

Her nipple hardened. and her groin felt watery.

"Know all about your daddy and what he done to your sister. Know about that fella you been whorin' with. Know all about you."

His thumb and forefinger tightened around her nipple.

Caroline closed her eyes tight.

"Look at me," he ordered, digging a fingernail into the pebbly, pink flesh.

The pain was excruciating, and, like a dumb animal, she obeyed.

"There ain't gonna be no more warnings after this. You tell him to quit nosin' around in matters that don't concern him."

CHAPTER THIRTY-FIVE

By tacit agreement, Andrusco's, a mob restaurant on Fifty-second Street near the East River, was like Switzerland: neutral territory, where people on both sides of the law could have a meal without business getting in the way. Every night except Monday, when it was shuttered, Andrusco's was packed with judges, politicians, and corporate heavies. The same people who fled from guys with names like Dman thought nothing of rubbing shoulders with the Frankie Sausages of the world. Life was indeed a mystery, Steeg reflected.

Richie Andrusco, a slope-shouldered, paunchy, middle-aged man with a bad toupee was the owner and resident host. Andrusco didn't take reservations. If he didn't know you personally, you didn't get in. If someone higher up in his pecking order showed up and the tables were all taken, Andrusco would unceremoniously roust someone lower down.

Steeg hated the place. Hated the heavy dark velvet draperies, the cheesy murals of happy gondoliers poling through Venice's canals, the forced bonhomie, and most of all, Richie Andrusco, who was a made guy and a stone killer in his own right. But it was Dave's show, and he went along with it.

Steeg and Dave were already seated when Dominic, wearing a baggy, gray, thirty-year-old double-breasted suit, arrived already half in the bag. It didn't go down well with Dave, but given the toxic circumstances, Steeg couldn't blame his father. The last time the three of them had been together was Norah's funeral. It took courage for Dominic to show up now, even if he had to find it at the bottom of a bottle of Bushmills. Steeg rose and pulled a chair out for him while Dave adjusted the knot of his tie and gave a distracted nod.

"Nice place," Dominic said, looking somewhat intimidated.

"I think it sucks, too, Pop." Steeg smiled, trying to ease the tension, but succeeding only in stoking Dave's coals.

The pebbly patch on Dave's cheek flared red. "Then let's get the fuck out of here and find a slop chute where you'd be more comfortable."

"Jesus Christ!" Steeg groaned. "Can't you lighten up?"

"This was your brilliant idea, remember?"

"Right, so don't screw it up," Steeg said.

Dominic's eyes moved from Steeg to Dave as if he were following the track of a tennis ball.

Just then, Richie Andrusco, his lips chiseled into a thin smile, magically appeared. He snapped his fingers and flagged down a waiter. "Hey, Gino, bring a bottle of Brunello, the ninety-nine." He turned back to Dave. "So, how's everybody doin' here?"

"Great," Dave said with a desultory wave of his hand.

"So," Andrusco persisted, stepping behind Dave and massaging the deltoids in his shoulders with his meaty hands. "You gonna introduce me to your friends?"

"We're not friends, we're family," Steeg said, with a straight face.

It took Richie a few seconds to catch the mood of the table. "Yeah, well, I know what that's all about. Someone's always pissed off about something." He removed his hands from Dave's shoulders and clasped them together in a prayerful gesture. "Nice meeting yez. Anything you need, just holler. By the way, the veal is terrific tonight. Just got a shipment in. Prepare it any way you want." He gave Dave's shoulders a last, therapeutic squeeze and moved on.

The wine came, and Steeg turned his glass upside down. The waiter poured for Dave and Dominic, dropped the menus, and left.

Dominic drank half of it while Dave, with a slight movement of his wrist, swirled the dark red liquid in his glass.

"It's all right," Dominic said, running his tongue over his lips. "But a little airy fairy for my tastes." He turned to Steeg. "I gotta hand it to you, Jake. Staying off the booze ain't easy. Your mother was always at me and I tried a couple of times, y'know, for her. Didn't work." He lifted the glass and finished the wine. "You think I could get a John Black, neat?"

"You were much better at doing things to her rather than for her," Dave said.

Steeg shook his head in frustration. He didn't object when Dave picked Andrusco's, figuring that it was too public for a scene. But Dave wasn't staying with the program. "Do you think we could maybe calm down a bit?"

Dominic ignored him. He turned to Dave. "What the hell's that supposed to mean?"

"In case I missed something, you were never up for Husband of the Year." Dave shook his head dismissively. "Ah, what's the use? Hey, Gino," he called to the waiter. "Two Blacks, neat."

The combination of the wine and whatever he had consumed earlier, turned Dominic's normally pale skin slack and lusterless and his eyes watery. "I always treated your mother with respect, so what's your problem? Look, I know maybe I was a little hard on you, and things kinda got out of hand sometimes, but you brought a lot of that stuff on yourself."

"This ain't about me," Dave said. "It's about Mom."

"What are you talking about?"

The waiter appeared with their drinks, took one look, and headed for a more congenial table.

Dominic downed it in one swallow and rapped the glass on the table for a refill. "Once and for all, let's get everything out in the open, okay? What the hell is bothering you all these years? I got grandchildren don't know I'm alive and a son who spits at the mention of my name." His voice was rising, and he was slurring his words. "I show up here to try to make things right and you . . . you piss all over me. It ain't right. Whyn't you just get it off your chest."

Dave eyes narrowed. His lips curled into a knowing smile. "Believe me, that's the last thing you want."

"I think I'm gonna have the veal piccatta," Steeg

said. "Anyone want to split an order of steamers?"

"Y'know why I was tough on you? 'Cause I didn't want you to turn out like you did."

People at other tables were beginning to stare.

"I was a cop, remember?" Dominic continued. "I seen lowlife little punks grow up into lowlife hoodlums, and I didn't want that for you. You were always quicker with your fists than your brain. And if it took the toe of my brogan to head you in the right direction . . . then that's what it took." He jerked a thumb in Steeg's direction. "He coulda used more of that, too, but your mother was always getting in the middle."

Dave smiled without mirth. "Worked like a charm, Pop."

Steeg just shook his head. Dominic never disappointed.

"Ain't my fault I got one son who's a bum and another who's going down the same road." He turned to look for a waiter. "Where's my fucking drink?" he shouted.

Dominic's wheels were coming off. He had reached the tipping point that every drunk arrived at just before he fell off the planet.

Richie Andrusco hurried over. His smile was hollow and flat. "Everything all right here?"

"No, it's not all right, you guinea fuck," Dominic said. "I need another drink."

Perfect, Steeg thought. Another lovely evening out with the family.

Andrusco's lips formed a thin, white line. His voice was low and hard. "You may be Dave's father, but you open your fuckin' trap again, you're gonna be on the street. Unnerstand?"

"You wop —!" Dominic tried to get up, but Dave reached across the table and grabbed him.

Dave looked up at Andrusco. "Beat it!"

Andrusco's eyes went dead. "What did you say?"

The ambient clatter of silverware on plates ceased.

"You heard me, fuck off. This is a family matter." He turned his attention back to Dominic, ignoring Andrusco.

A muscle twitched like a live wire in the hinge of Andrusco's jaw.

Steeg, expecting an eruption, carefully watched him.

But Andrusco surprised him. In an instant he was all smiles, nodding and winking at customers, but backing off.

"That was close," Steeg said.

"No, it wasn't," Dave replied. "You had my back."

"What were we talking about?" Dominic said, trying to rub memory back into his brain.

"What a wonderful dad you were," Dave said.

"Oh, right. My boys. So much to be proud of." He wiped his nose on his jacket sleeve. "Ain't my fault. Did all I could, but your mother got between us. You, especially, Dave, you she coddled."

"Protected me from you is more like it."

Dominic leveled him with a withering look. "And I protected you from yourself."

"What's that supposed to mean?"

Dominic turned away. "Nothing. It was always you and your mother, never any room for me. What's the difference, you were always a momma's boy, anyway."

The magic words! Steeg braced for the explosion.

"*Momma's boy?*" Dave repeated. He threw his napkin on the table and leaped to his feet. The tendons in his neck bulged like steel cables.

Dominic looked at him with incomprehension.

Dave's hand went to his pants pocket and came out with a thick wad of bills. He peeled several off and threw them on the table. "I'm outta here," he said. He turned to Dominic. "The next time I see you, it'll be your funeral."

Steeg got to his feet and threw his arms around Dave in a bear hug. "Come on, Dave, he's drunk. Doesn't know what he's saying."

He shrugged Steeg off. "You give him too much credit. After all these years, he still knows what buttons to push. I'll be in touch."

Through bleary eyes, Dominic watched Dave leave. "Once a bum, always a bum. No respect. Good riddance! Now, where's my drink?"

"You're cut off."

Dominic bristled. "Who said?"

"I did."

He bowed his head and ran his fingers through his hair. "Not much, am I?"

"When you're a kid, you think life is supposed to be a television show," Steeg said. "A place that's perfect. But when you shut the TV off and look around —"

"It's a whole different world."

"Yeah," Steeg said.

"I loved you boys, just like I loved your mother."

"But what happened?"

Dominic recoiled as if he had been slapped. "Let's talk about other things."

"Sure."

"How's your investigation going?"

"It's not. I've learned some things, but I'm still hammering my head against the wall."

Dominic's gaze became dreamy, as if it were dredging for long-buried memories. "She was something special, that one." His voice grew soft. "She made it out of the Kitchen, and what did it get her?"

"Who, Diana? She wasn't from here. Fifth Avenue all the way."

With the pads of his fingers, Dominic rubbed color into his cheeks. "Not Diana . . . Linda."

Steeg threw a quizzical glance at Dominic. "Linda Strickland was from Hell's Kitchen?"

Dominic reddened. "Who? Linda? No . . . I meant the daughter."

"But you said Linda."

"I got . . . confused." He struggled to his feet. "Look, I'm not feeling too well, gotta get home. Can't handle as much as I used to. Get me a cab."

Steeg got to his feet and took Dominic's arm. "I'll take you. It's only a few blocks."

A fine sheen of perspiration sprang to his forehead, his skin looked jaundiced. "You know the feeling, ain't gonna make it. Gotta go or I'll be sick all over myself."

Steeg got him out of the restaurant and into a cab waiting in front.

"I'll go with you."

"Don't need your help," Dominic mumbled. "Don't . . . need anyone's help anymore."

When he arrived home there was one message waiting on Steeg's answering machine.

"Oh God, he was . . . here! I'm leaving. Don't know where I'm going, but I have to get out of here. He had a message for you. Drop it, Steeg. Whatever you're doing . . . just drop it and run!

Steeg lifted the phone and punched in Caroline's number. There was no answer.

CHAPTER THIRTY-SIX

It was a drunk's truth.

All of us have a place where we store our sins. To keep a hold on sanity, we bury them in the dark, cold place where the snakes sleep and we spend our waking hours trying to keep the lid on, tight. Straights are fairly successful at keeping the demons at bay, rarely having to confront the pain of revelation. Drunks are not. The bugs crawling through their brains eat through the wiring and pop the lid on Pandora's box. And that's exactly what had happened to Dominic. In one unguarded moment, something that he had buried a long time ago flew into the sunlight.

If Dominic was right, Linda Strickland had achieved her version of the American dream — the Hell's Kitchen moth metamorphosing into a Social Register butterfly. She should have been more careful about what she wished for. Prince Charming turned out to be a toad, and she wound up facedown on Fifth Avenue.

It was time to check Dominic's story.

As a child, Steeg had spent too much involuntary time in Monsignor Tom Fallon's office in the rectory of the

Church of the Precious Blood. On those occasions when he had worn the nuns' patience down to a nub, Fallon's office was the final stop on the bumpy road to contrition. Wearing a scowl like it was part of his uniform, he was an intimidating presence. Tall and beefy, with bushy eyebrows and hands the size of dinner plates, Fallon was definitely not your basic Hollywood-style kindly priest with twinkling eyes and a warm smile. He wielded a heavy ruler and unforgiving justice with equal efficiency. The years had not been particularly kind. The beef had turned to fat, the eyebrows had turned gray and spiky, and jowls hung loosely over his turned-around collar.

Fallon peered at Steeg through watery eyes. "My, my! Whoever said there aren't miracles anymore is a fool. I never thought I'd see you here again."

"Spoken like a true man of faith."

The sour expression on Fallon's face told Steeg that his witty repartee was singularly unappreciated.

"God help me for admitting it, but I never did like you," Fallon said. "You were always an odd child. Too cocksure. Marched to the sound of your own drummer. Never went along to get along."

"An opinion shared by many."

"No doubt. Why are you here?"

"It's a long shot, but I think you can help me."

"Must I ask the obvious?" He paused. "Why should I help you?"

Steeg smiled. "Because it's in your job description?"

Fallon nodded. He reached for a pack of Marlboros, tapped one out, and placed it between his lips. "Can't have them anymore." He touched his chest. "Bad ticker.

But it still feels good in my mouth." Chewing on the filter, he gazed out of the window. "Your father was in this morning. Makes Mass pretty regularly. You're always in his prayers."

"Pop's a spiritual guy."

He turned back to Steeg. "But not you."

"Not me," Steeg admitted.

"And why is that?"

"If Christ came back and saw the things we do to each other, it would make Him weep."

Fallon pulled the cigarette from his lips and ground it into an ashtray. "What do you want to know?"

"I'm looking for a girl who might have been a member of this parish at least forty years ago, probably more. It's possible she attended the school."

"You'd be better off searching for the Grail."

"That's next on my list."

Fallon let out a weary sigh. "Does she have a name?"

"Linda, and I'm not even sure it's her real name. Strickland was her married name."

The color drained from Fallon's face. He answered too quickly. "Doesn't ring a bell."

It was like watching an elephant negotiate a high wire. Deception didn't come easy to this man of the cloth. "I'm investigating her murder. Look, I know she was from Hell's Kitchen. One day she picked up and left, assumed a new identity, became a fashion model, and married into a very wealthy family. I'm guessing about the Catholic part, but given the religious makeup of the Kitchen forty years ago, I don't think I'm far off."

The color slowly returned to Fallon's face. His gaze

drifted skyward as if the answer were written on the ceiling. "I'll ask around. Some of the older sisters may remember her." He stroked his chin and forced a smile. "Why don't you call me in a few days."

"I'll do that."

"I'm curious. How long has it been since your last confession?"

Steeg got up to leave. "How long has it been since yours, Father?"

Fallon looked away and reached for another Marlboro. His other hand went into his cassock and came out with a book of matches. He ripped one off and struck it, touching the flame to the tip of the cigarette. He inhaled deeply. "Good luck with your search, my son. In the meanwhile, I'll pray for you."

Steeg left the rectory and wandered into the church, looking not for absolution but a place to think. It was empty, and he settled into a pew near the back. Fallon was lying. Why, Steeg didn't know, but he was lying. Precious Blood was his first assignment after he'd graduated from seminary, and Fallon had served the parish long enough to know every family. He had to have known Linda, so why was he covering it up? And how about Linda? Many people wear their humble origins like a badge of honor. But not Linda. Who or what was she running from?

Assuming a new identity is always a dangerous game — the past has a funny way of barging in and screwing things up when you least expect it. It was possible that someone with knowledge of Linda's past had tried to earn a few bucks through extortion. After a while,

Linda could have had enough and threatened to go to the police. Plausible? Absolutely. But finding that person was another story. It could have been anyone, a Hell's Kitchen lowlife, or a former enemy out for revenge. But, Steeg thought, why kill her daughter over twenty years later? That connection shortened the list of suspects, but it was a wrinkle that Steeg didn't have any theories to account for.

Steeg smelled him before he heard his voice, a moist, sour odor reminiscent of untreated sewage.

"Don't turn around," Floyd said.

Something cold and metallic jabbed at the base of Steeg's skull. "I was wondering when you would show up."

Floyd's voice was low. "I bet you was."

"What do you want?"

"How's the child?"

It took a few seconds before Steeg realized that Floyd was asking about DeeDee. "She's good, but Dman is another story. It's gonna be years till he does the Macarena again. I owe you for what you did."

"You don't owe me anythin', but I 'ppreciate the thought."

"Who sent you, Samael? Who're you working for?"

"Why'd you sic your dogs on me?"

"What are you talking about?"

"They don't give me no peace. Everywhere I look, people are tryin' to kill me. It ain't neighborly, pilgrim."

Dave's guys had him running, and Floyd was wound tighter than a guitar string. "That sometimes happens in your line of work, an occupational hazard."

"Don't matter, they're dead. Won't be botherin' no one no more."

"How come I'm not dead? God knows you had your chances."

"God loves the steadfast and true, Mr. Steeg."

"Then I should have been gone a long time ago."

"Maybe, but it wasn't my call. Anyway, I come to say good-bye. Time to move on. Got one more visit to make and then I'm gone."

Steeg started to turn, but the object pressed against the base of his skull dug in deeper.

"Not a good idea," Floyd said. "Anyway, that's all I got to say."

"So, that's it."

"'Pears to be. The Lord is far from the wicked, but he heareth the prayers of the righteous. If you come to a violent end, it ain't gonna be by my hand."

"What changed?"

"I seen you with that little girl and it kind of reoriented my thinkin'. It counts for somethin'."

"You didn't answer my question. Who sent you?"

"I owe you that much, pilgrim." He brought his mouth so close to Steeg's ear he felt the rough stubble of Floyd's cheek on the back of his neck. "It was Esau that sent me," he whispered.

"I don't understand."

"Lots of sins to be atoned for."

The pressure on the back of Steeg's head eased. Steeg turned and Floyd was gone.

CHAPTER THIRTY-SEVEN

Steeg put Floyd's blatherings down to the ravings of a lunatic. Esau was probably another inhabitant of the seething brew he called a brain. But, as often happens, one man's insanity is another man's inspiration. He left the church, pulled out his cell phone, and punched in Luce's number. She answered on the first ring.

"Hello?" she said.

"It's me. Remember a while back I asked you to get me Linda Strickland's file?"

"I'm really tired of doin' this, Jackson. You really have to learn how to carry on a conversation like a normal person. As empty and insincere as it is, I say 'hello' and you say 'hello.' Then I ask about your health, and you do the same. It's really easy to remember."

"Fine! Hello, how are you, where's the file?"

"That's much better. How's DeeDee?"

"Good. Now where's —" Steeg paused. "How's Cherise?"

"Good. I always said you were a quick study. I mailed it to you right after you asked. Should be on the desk underneath all them bills."

"Why didn't you tell me you had mailed it?"

"'Cause I ain't your mother," she said, hanging up.

He hurried home and found the envelope where Luce said it would be. He picked it up and took it into the kitchen. He retrieved a can of Coke from the fridge and spread the file out on the table.

For a high-profile case, the file was surprisingly sparse. The M.E.'s report was there, along with Dominic's black leather notepads detailing his interviews with the doorman, Linda's neighbors, and Earl Strickland. Conspicuously missing was his interview with Diana. This was strange. Unlike Steeg, Dominic was a stickler for procedure, and an investigating Detective's notes are always included in the file. Given that Diana had claimed to see her mother's murderer, the absence of the interview notes didn't add up. His curiosity piqued, he picked up the phone and called Dominic. He got his answering machine instead. Steeg left a message and went back to the file.

Earl's interview had been short and sweet. With an alibi as solid as his, there really wasn't much to say. At the exact time that Linda took a header off the balcony, Earl was attending a meeting of the board of the Metropolitan Opera. Also in attendance was the mayor, the president of the City Council, and assorted rich folks. It was enough to eliminate Earl as a suspect. As a motive, blackmail was looking better and better.

The half-lidded eyes, the inverted half-moon of his mouth, and the weak line of his jaw all conspired to give Lenny Roberts the appearance of a gentle, plodding man of low intelligence.

Joey Rizzo knew better.

Roberts sat in Rizzo's chair with his black, tasseled loafers propped on the desk. Rizzo was on the sofa opposite him, nursing a single-malt scotch.

Roberts plucked a piece of lint from his navy blue blazer and flicked it on the floor. "Where'd the long-legged gal with the big tits disappear with my drink?"

Rizzo reached for the phone and punched few numbers. After a few seconds, he slammed the phone down. "Fuckin' whore! I'll go check," he said.

"No, that's all right. She'll be along." He paused. "I got some news," Roberts said, gently patting a helmet of hair that appeared to have been lacquered on.

Rizzo remained silent.

"You did a good job here, Joey, customers are happy, business is good. Real good. Over the next twelve months we're going to be opening a new Pinky's in Boston, Chicago, and Los Angeles. And as soon as Sloan gets his new building up here, we're moving in." He paused. "And I'm putting you in charge of it all. How does that sound?"

Rizzo took a sip of whiskey and leaned back. "Opportunity of a lifetime."

Roberts smiled. "Got so many girls coming in from Eastern Europe and Asia, I've got to open more clubs just to give them a place to work. Let the Colombians screw with drugs." He laughed. "These gals are a replenishable commodity."

"And you don't have the DEA crawlin' up your ass," Rizzo said.

He swung his feet to the floor and pulled the chair

up to the desk. "I want you to start thinking about your replacement, and I want you on a plane next week to scout locations. Okay?"

Before Rizzo had a chance to reply, the door swung open and Floyd filled the doorway. He smelled rank. His hair was matted and dirty, and his black eyes glowed with an ethereal light.

Rizzo went white. "How the fuck did you get in here?"

Roberts kept his voice low and soothing, carefully avoiding setting off Floyd's tripwires. He had a healthy respect for Floyd, the only man whose capacity for violence exceeded his own. "Hey, Samael. How're you doing?"

"The house of the wicked shall be overthrown, but the tabernacle of the righteous shall flourish."

The Indian was still riding the Jesus train, Roberts thought.

Rizzo pointed a nubby finger at Floyd. "Listen —!"

Roberts cut him off. "You have no business here Samael, and I'd appreciate it if you leave."

"Can't do that," Floyd said. "It's time to settle up. Make the accounts straight."

Roberts reached into his pants pocket and pulled out a roll of bills. "If it's money you need, you —"

Floyd walked over and slapped the money out of Roberts's hand. "Filthy lucre! And don't be thinkin' about pressin' that little button under the desk. Ain't gonna do you no good. There'll be no help comin' today. From here on in, it's just the three of us."

A fine sheen of perspiration appeared on Roberts's face. "What do you want, Samael?"

"Blood," he said.

Rizzo jumped to his feet. "That's it, Cochise! You just stepped into a world of shit. Do you know who you're fuckin' with, you crazy bastard?"

With a move that was too quick to follow, Floyd backhanded him, slamming him into the sofa and driving his nose into his brain.

Floyd turned his attention to Roberts. "I thought we were friends. Why'd you put your gunmen on me?"

Roberts stared at Floyd, wide-eyed. With growing awareness, he knew how this would play out. His sphincter loosened, filling the room with a fetid odor. "We're friends. I never did that," he cried. "You know me, I'd never —"

Floyd walked over to Roberts and gently put his hand over his mouth. "Hushhh!" he said. The sound was like the hissing of a snake. "Deceit is in the heart of them that devise evil." With his free hand he opened the desk drawer, reached in, and pulled out Rizzo's .38.

Roberts's hands flew to his face as Floyd spun and fired. A small hole appeared in Rizzo's forehead. He turned back to Roberts.

"Please," Roberts begged. "Please don't —" A thin, yellowish stream of spittle ran down his chin.

Floyd's voice rose to a shout. "The mouth of the wicked poureth out evil things," he said, jamming the muzzle into Roberts's mouth and pulling the trigger.

CHAPTER THIRTY-EIGHT

Steeg had spent a fitful night and rose late. He missed the women who had lately populated his life and he missed Herkie. He had tried his father's number several times without any luck. It wasn't surprising. Dominic had dived so far into the bottle, it would take the Jaws of Life to pull him out. The thought of inviting him to an AA meeting crossed Steeg's mind: but he quickly dismissed it; public displays of personal weakness wasn't Dominic's style.

He ate breakfast and looked out the kitchen window. It was 10:00 a.m., and the morning was drenched with sunlight. It was as if a switch had been tripped in Steeg's brain. Suddenly, his long-dormant muscles ached for exercise. He went into the bedroom and threw on his NYPD sweatshirt and a pair of running shorts, laced up his sneakers, and set off for the river. From Midtown to the Battery was a little over three miles, if his legs could take it. With a wall of traffic to his left and a string of piers to his right, Steeg set off at an easy pace, synchronizing his stride to the beating of his heart.

For nearly fifty years, the elevated structure of the West Side Highway had separated the Hudson River shoreline from the interior of Manhattan. After years of benign neglect, in 1973 a cement truck fell through a deteriorating sixty-foot section it was sent to repair. The great cosmic joke turned out to be a gift. The grimy, blighted stretch of elevated highway was transformed into a wide boulevard, offering some of the most spectacular views of the city.

Once past the USS *Intrepid* and the Circle Line cruise wharf, Steeg had an unobstructed view of the Hudson. The sunlight reflecting off the river made it appear as if diamonds were strewn on its surface. Just off the New Jersey shore, a flock of wheeling gulls dove into a shoal of baitfish.

Steeg kicked into a sprint. Dark blotches of sweat stained his shirt. He flew past the Meatpacking District and Chelsea Piers, and it wasn't until he reached the West Village that he slowed to a stop. Bending over and resting his hands on his knees, he waited until his breathing had returned to normal. So absorbed was he in the rhythms of his body, he failed to notice the car that had pulled up beside him.

"Hey, Steeg!"

The blood roaring in his ears set against the blare of the traffic made it impossible for him hear.

The passenger door opened, and a man climbed out. He walked over to Steeg.

Still bent over, Steeg saw the thick-soled shoes and pegged him for a cop. He straightened up.

"Lou Gangemi." He smiled. "What a pleasant surprise."

"Fuck you, too, Steeg. Braddock wants to see you."

Steeg pulled his sweatshirt over his head and used it to mop his face. "Tell him it's my day off," he said, preparing to resume his run.

Gangemi locked his hand on Steeg's wrist. "Don't be such a ballbreaker, okay?"

"I would really think about letting go, if I were you."

Gangemi released his grip. "Look, he's in the car over there and he just wants a few minutes of your time. C'mon, I never did anything to you, never fucked you, so don't make me look bad."

Steeg was very familiar with the "Don't Make Me Look Bad" rule. But he also knew that when cops covered for each other, only bad things happened. But, in this case, he made an exception. Gangemi was harmless. He followed him to the unmarked.

Gangemi opened the rear door and motioned for Steeg to get in.

Braddock was all smiles. Wearing a navy blue, wrinkle-free Sears suit and a matching tie, Braddock looked like a used-car salesman.

"Good to see you," he said, clapping Steeg on the shoulder. "How've you been doing?"

"How'd you know where to find me?"

"Its my business to know where you are."

Braddock confirmed what Luce had said. He glanced at the front seat and was surprised to see Petrovitch behind the wheel.

"Hey, Wayne, how's it hanging? Beat the shit out of any handcuffed guys today?"

Petrovitch stared out the windshield.

Steeg turned to Braddock. "What's he doing here?"

Braddock flashed a set of off-white crooked teeth in a pasted-on smile. "It's part of the reason I'm here. See, uh, it's like this."

Steeg noticed that the words weren't coming easily to Braddock.

Braddock continued. "There's been a misunderstanding . . . and though there's enough fault to go around, the buck stops with me. Right?"

"I'm not too clear about the 'fault' part."

"I've reexamined the circumstances leading up to your suspension and . . . while your, uh, behavior was somewhat questionable, it was understandable, and Sergeant Petrovitch agrees. Right, Wayne?

Petrovitch continued to stare through the windshield. "Yeah."

"In fact, he'd like to offer you his apologies."

Braddock turned to look at the back of Petrovitch's head.

"Sorry," Petrovitch said.

Braddock turned back to Steeg. "There, that's settled. What do you think?"

"Touching and heartfelt. Brought tears to my eyes."

"There's more good news," Braddock said.

"I can hardly wait."

Braddock's smile froze, but he continued. "Your suspension is over, and I've had it stricken from your record like it never existed."

Steeg jerked his chin in Petrovitch's direction. "What about the asshole, is he off the hook?"

Petrovitch swung around with his eyes blazing. "I'm gonna kill ya, ya bastard! Count on it."

Braddock stopped him before he had a chance to latch on to Steeg's throat. "*Wayne!* Wait outside with Gangemi."

Petrovitch didn't like it, but he didn't have much choice in the matter.

"Sensitive sort, isn't he?" Steeg said.

Braddock's smile was gone. "All right, fuckwit, it's just the two of us. Let me play it out for you. This wasn't my idea."

"If it had been, it would have been a first. What's going on, Gerry?"

"What's going on is well above my pay grade. I got a call to make everything go away, so I did."

"From who?"

"The Commissioner."

"And why would the Commissioner be interested in insignificant old me?"

"Because he got a phone call from the mayor, who got a call from the head of the City Council, who got a —"

Steeg completed the sentence. "Call from Terry Sloan and Gideon El."

"Bingo!"

"Why?"

"Because they're scared shitless. In fact, we're going to see them now, so you can hear it from the horses' mouths."

CHAPTER THIRTY-NINE

The news media was three deep outside the Hudson Democratic Club. Braddock, with Steeg in tow, elbowed his way through the crowd.

"What's going on?" Steeg said.

"A press conference."

Braddock led him through the empty club into Terry Sloan's office. Sloan, Mallus, and Gideon El had the look of men peering into the abyss.

"Thanks for coming," Sloan said.

"I didn't have much choice," Steeg replied.

"I don't know if you heard, but there's been more killings. Lenny Roberts and Joey Rizzo."

"And three of their employees," Mallus added.

"I'd say the mayor's initiative on urban pollution is succeeding," Steeg said.

"This is not funny," Gideon El interjected. "The community is frightened, and I don't blame them. That's why the press is here. We're here to calm the community down, and the only way we do that is by assuring everyone that we're ahead of the curve on this one."

"What does that mean?" Steeg said.

"Look, Jake," Sloan said. "We have every reason to believe that your lunatic Indian is behind this."

"And you know this how?"

Mallus folded his arms across his chest and threw Steeg a look. "Because we have witnesses. He beat three steroid freaks to death with his bare hands, a feat he nearly accomplished with Dman. And then painted the walls with Roberts's and Rizzo's brains."

"What's that got to do with me?"

Sloan answered for the group. "Everyone around you seems to wind up dead or in intensive care, except you. We find that curious."

"Funny, I find it life-affirming."

"Our sources tell us that you're the one he was after, but somehow things got twisted all around. Something made him change his mind, and other people wound up dead. Why is that, do you think?"

"I never realized it until now, but you have a very dark view of people, Terry. Perhaps Floyd was exhibiting the human capacity for change. You know, evolving."

"I told you this was a waste of time," Mallus said.

Steeg was bored with the fun and games. "Why am I here?"

"Call the psycho off," Sloan said.

"You think he's working for *me*?"

"Who the hell knows? Look, he's fucking up our Riverview project. With all the killings, the area is getting a bad rap and prospective tenants are staying away in droves. Federal and state money is in danger of being pulled. Who wants to tiptoe over corpses on their way into work? The other thing we're wondering is when he's going to come after us."

"And why would he do that?"

"Because he's done it to everyone else you know."

"Did he do Herkie?"

"Who?"

"John Herkimer, a homeless guy. My friend."

"We think so," Braddock said.

"If I remember, there were some other homeless guys killed around the same time. Part of the urban cleanup for Riverview?"

"No," Braddock said. "It was Dman's crew, just boys wanting to have fun."

Steeg nodded. "Listen, fellas, I hate to bust your bubble, but Floyd isn't working for me. But you don't have to worry about Floyd anymore. He's not coming after you."

"What's that supposed to mean?" Sloan said.

"He told me he was leaving."

"And you believe him?"

"More than I believe you."

CHAPTER FORTY

Steeg was worried. Since he had left Sloan and his gang of miscreants, he had called Dominic twice and still got no response. Something was definitely wrong. He hurried over to Dominic's building and ran up the three flights, taking the stairs two at a time.

Breathing hard, he knocked on the door. "Pop, are you there?" Silence. He knocked again, harder. Nothing. He ran downstairs to find the super. Apartment 1A, the registry said. He rang the bell. A gray-haired black man wearing a white T-shirt and jeans came to the door, brushing some loose crumbs from his mouth.

"Yeah?" he said.

"I need to get into Dominic Steeg's apartment. I'm his son."

"Never seen you before," he said, closing the door.

Steeg grabbed the doorknob. "Trust me, there's something wrong. I need you to let me in."

"Maybe Mr. Steeg is out shopping or something."

"Stop busting my chops. Either you let me in or I kick the door down."

The super eyed him suspiciously. "Got any I.D.?"

Wonderful, Steeg thought. I'm dealing with the only super on Manhattan Island who gives a shit about security. He pulled out his wallet and flashed his driver's license.

The super's gaze flitted from the photo back to Steeg several times. "Never knew he had any children," he said, passing the wallet back to Steeg. "Never talked about you."

"He didn't like to brag. Now, can we get going?"

"Give me a moment," he said, disappearing into the apartment.

In a few seconds, he returned. "Okay, let's go." Steeg followed him up the stairs.

The super knocked on the door. "Mr. Steeg, it's Ernie. Are you there?"

Frowning, he turned to Steeg. "I don't like this, and Mr. Steeg ain't gonna like it when he finds out we've been in his apartment."

"You're off the hook, Ernie. Open it up."

Ernie slipped the key into the lock. He turned it, and the tumblers fell into place.

"I'll take it from here," Steeg said.

"The hell you will. The landlord makes the rules and he says that I gotta go with you."

Ernie swung the door open and walked in ahead of him. Steeg knew what he would find.

"Holy shit! You better get in here."

Steeg walked into the living room and saw Dominic slumped back in his chair. What appeared to be letters were strewn at his feet like so many dead leaves. In the midst of them was a black, leather-bound notebook. Dominic's service revolver was clenched in his right hand. The back of his head was pasted to the wall.

Steeg wasn't surprised. A sad and weary numbness settled over him.

"My God! Ain't never seen nothing like this before. This is a good building." Ernie brought out his cell phone. "Gotta call the cops."

Steeg snatched it out of his hand. He went for his wallet and fished out his NYPD I.D. and flashed it. "I *am* the cops." He took Ernie's arm and led him to the kitchen. "Here's what's gonna happen. You take a seat while I check around. Okay?"

With the hem of his T-shirt, Ernie mopped his forehead and nodded.

"I'm sure there's beer in the refrigerator, so make yourself comfortable and stay out of the living room. It's now officially a crime scene and I can't have you contaminating it."

Ernie rested his large hands on the table and nodded. "I liked him, y'know. Always did right by me."

Steeg patted his shoulder. "I'll be back in a few minutes, then we'll talk."

He walked into the living room and let first impressions wash over him.

Everything was neat, in its place; exactly how Norah would have kept it. His gaze moved to Dominic, noting the fresh haircut, the astringent odor of the aftershave lotion, the sharp crease of his uniform, the shoes polished to a high gloss, the gold Detective's shield pinned to his breast.

There was no suicide note, but Steeg sensed that Dominic was trying to communicate something nevertheless, something he was incapable of committing to paper.

Steeg knelt and randomly plucked a letter from the floor. The paper was dry and brittle, and the ink was fading. It was written with fluid, precise strokes on expensive stationery. He read it and felt his excitement mounting. He lowered himself to the floor and gathered all the letters into a stack. Sitting cross-legged, he arranged them in chronological order. There were twenty letters in all, spanning nineteen years, and they were all from Linda Strickland.

The first was addressed to Dominic while he was serving in the army. It appeared to have been crumpled once, but Dominic had done his best to smooth it out. It was a Dear John letter. She loved him and would always love him, she had said, but it wasn't going to work. She wanted more out of life than a life in Hell's Kitchen. She closed by wishing him well and asked that he not try to contact her.

Steeg remembered that Dominic had enlisted right after high school. He was eighteen, and she was probably the same age or younger. They were babies.

The next letter was dated ten years later. Dominic had received a commendation for bravery from the police department. The newspapers had covered the ceremony, and Dominic's photo made the front page. Linda had seen it. She'd told him that she was proud of him and happy that his career was going well. In the lower-left corner she had written her phone number. Steeg did a quick calculation. Dominic and Norah had been married for eight years. Dave was seven, and he was one.

Most of the other letters were mostly chatty, filled with the mundane things people with an easy relationship talk about. They were written from Linda's perspective but they revealed much about Dominic. As children often do, Steeg had had a one-dimensional view of Dominic. It wasn't until now that he saw him as a man with all the complexities and foibles that men have. It was a jarring awakening.

There was one letter left, and Steeg picked it up. When he finished reading, he realized that everything had come full circle. It was a response to his Dear John letter to her. Linda was pregnant and wanted to leave Earl and marry Dominic. But Dominic had refused. To destroy two families was unthinkable. Reluctantly, she had agreed with his decision to end their relationship for good.

Steeg placed the letter on top of the others and sat quietly for a few minutes, ordering his thoughts. Dominic had loved Linda and he had loved his own family too. There was no right and no wrong, only a man tangled in the web of circumstances that he himself had woven.

But why had it led to suicide? Steeg hadn't figured that out yet.

Steeg heard Ernie moving about in the kitchen. He was running out of time. He reached for the notepad and slipped it in his jacket pocket.

He got to his feet and took in the scene one more time and, in a burst of clarity, he knew what Dominic was trying to tell him. There would be no written suicide note; Dominic was too private a person for that. Rather, the entire scene was designed for Steeg. In it, Dominic had laid out the alphabet of his life, and the reason for his death. It was now up to Steeg to find the truth in the white spaces.

Steeg gathered up the letters and notebook, and stuffed them in his jacket pocket. In his haste to leave, he almost missed the final piece of the puzzle. Wedged between Dominic's thigh and the chair's armrest was another letter. He gently eased it out and read it.

CHAPTER FORTY-ONE

Dominic's wake was a raucous affair. Sal Matarazzo catered it, and a bunch of Dominic's old buddies came to see him off. They wore somber suits and dour expressions, and no one spoke ill of the dead. And when they got into the free booze, it turned into an old-time Department racket. Until now, Steeg would have viewed the ritual with a skeptic's arched eyebrow and peeled eye. But things had changed, not necessarily for the good because there was no good to be found anywhere, but things were different now. Their send-off was a tribute to the warmth, humor, and generosity of spirit of a man he and Dave had never known. They were all looking at the elephant from different sides.

Franny and DeeDee and the kids had shown up, but Dave had not. Franny was too embarrassed to offer a reason for his absence. It was better that he wasn't there; Steeg wasn't ready see him yet. DeeDee sat with him and asked when she could come home. At least one thing was going right in his life.

The Garden of the Holy Rest covered a hundred acres of gently rolling Long Island countryside that had once been used to grow potatoes. The trees were beginning to bud, and their branches were covered with a pale green haze.

At Steeg's request, only the immediate family was invited to the graveside service. It took about twenty minutes. Monsignor Fallon's eulogy included the usual pious platitudes lauding Dominic's sterling qualities as a husband, a father, and a protector of the community. Dave's expression said he didn't believe a word of it. He stood apart from the group with his hand on Norah's tombstone, impatiently waiting for Fallon to wind it down.

Having run out of his store of encomiums, with a final sprinkle of Holy Water and a hurried prayer, Fallon announced that the service was over. Embracing everyone but Steeg, he got in his car and left.

Steeg turned to Franny. "Do you mind waiting in the car with DeeDee and the kids? I want to talk to my brother."

She threw her arms around Steeg and hugged him. Her eyes were wet. "It's a complicated thing, Jake, but Dave loved him, I know he did."

He kissed her forehead. "We won't be very long."

She nodded and walked over to the children.

Steeg found Dave at Norah's tombstone. He knelt and brushed some dead leaves from between the junipers. "Let's take a walk," Steeg said.

"What's on your mind?"

"I'd rather not talk about it here."

"I don't mind — say what you gotta say."

"Why did you do it?"

Dave looked down at the grave and ran his fingers over the smooth surface of the granite.

Steeg heard the harsh rasping sound of the shovels and looked at Dominic's grave. The coffin was covered with dirt.

Dave looked over at Franny and the kids. He took Steeg's arm.

They walked along a winding path, past carvings of angels and praying hands. Steeg waited until they were safely out of earshot before he broke the silence. "Dominic and Linda Strickland were lovers, but you knew that. Dominic had saved her letters all these years."

Dave's gaze drifted into the distance above the tree line to a point on the horizon.

Steeg continued. "They met when they were kids. Her name was Stearnes, Linda Stearnes. She was from Hell's Kitchen."

"You're a good cop, Jake."

Steeg's eyes locked on Dave's. "And you're a murderer."

Dave's face tightened.

"They were in love long before Norah came into the picture," Steeg said. "The kind of love that gives teenagers night sweats."

"It's hard imagining any woman, including your mother, in love with your father," Dave said, his voice sounding as far away as his gaze.

The white contrails of a 747 etched clean lines in the sky. Dave looked at it like it was marking the road to Heaven.

"I saw them together," Dave said. "A sporting goods store on Second Avenue in the Sixties. Was owned by some baseball player who came up to the majors for a cup of coffee and was never heard from again."

Steeg remained silent.

"We were gonna do a heist and I was checking it out. There was this fancy restaurant next door. I look in the window and the two of them are holding hands." He turned back to Steeg, his mouth twisted into a snarl. "If I had my piece, I would have blown their fucking heads off."

"So you did the next-best thing. You murdered her."

Dave shrugged, and his features softened. "I heard there's something called a butterfly bush. Pretty flowers, lavender pink, and the butterflies just swarm all over them." He paused and looked down. "I did it for Norah."

Steeg's lips tightened into a thin white line. "No, you did it for you. It's all on you. You appointed yourself judge, jury, and executioner, and it was none of your goddamn business. You didn't know what went on in Norah and Dominic's marriage any more than I know what goes on in yours." Steeg grabbed Dave's shoulders. "Dominic was just a guy, no different from other men. No different from you or me."

Dave pulled away. "Never once did I raise my voice or my hand to my wife or my kids." He rapped his fist against his chest. "I was a better man," he insisted.

"Do you realize how insane that sounds? The sad thing is, you're not better, not even close."

"Bullshit!"

"For a man who claims that nothing matters more than family, you wound up destroying two; *he* didn't."

"You bastard!" Dave screamed. He spun, and his fist caught Steeg squarely on the temple.

Steeg never saw it coming. He staggered back, dazed. Blood ran down his cheek.

He gently touched the wound. It was beginning to swell. "You tracked her until you figured a way into her apartment. Said you were the plumber."

Dave's eyes widened with surprise, but his voice was hollow. "Manzi Brothers. Plumber's assistant. Dominic got me the job."

"I know. There was a witness . . . a frightened little girl who saw you throw her mother off the balcony. Dominic had it in his little black book. She remembered that the killer wore a green uniform with big red letters on the back. Dominic put two and two together. He knew you killed Linda, but he couldn't turn his son in."

"I gotta sit down," Dave said. His voice sounded weary and confused.

They found a stone bench under the branches of a maple tree. Steeg wanted it to end here, but he couldn't.

Dave hung his head in his hands. "Remember the butterflies, Jake? Ivar and Brian and the butterflies beating their wings and moving the sun? It was a miracle, a happy ending, and I wanted the same the thing for us. I thought he was going to leave Norah, and I couldn't let that happen. We were a family, damn it! Fucked up, but it was all I had. After all Norah had done for me, I couldn't let it happen. You're right, I couldn't kill him, but I could kill the thing he loved most, and make the son of a bitch spend the rest of his life in the kind of pain he caused Norah . . . and me."

Steeg stared at him. "And where did I figure in all this?"

"Blame the whore's daughter. Fuckin' Moore made a mistake. I didn't know he lived in your building."

Steeg's voice rose. "Why kill her? She was a baby when it happened. She couldn't read the name on your uniform!"

"It wasn't my uniform." Dave brought his fingers to his cheek. "It was my *face!*"

"What?"

"The port-wine stain. In some junkie haze, she remembered. She told Moore, and it got back to me because even though I never met her, I was running her. Me and Roberts. She was like a novelty fuck, a Fifth Avenue socialite banging anyone with a few bucks in his pocket. She started with Terry and worked her way through Gideon El and Mallus. Hell, they traded her around like a baseball card. She was a junkie with a big mouth and a memory, and I couldn't let her live. And then you show up and get curious."

"So you hired Floyd."

"How did you know?"

"Floyd tipped me. He said Esau had sent him. At first, I didn't know what he was talking about. But the more I thought about it, the more I realized I had heard the name before. Remember what Norah left me when she passed?"

Dave clenched his teeth, and the muscles in his jaw jumped. "Her Bible."

Steeg nodded. "I looked him up. He and Jacob were brothers. It says that Esau was a mighty hunter. A man

249

covered with blood. Jacob spent his life worried that Esau would kill him."

Dave studied his fingernails. "But he didn't. I got the Indian through Roberts. I'm not proud of that, but you weren't supposed to get hurt, just scared. Hell, the crazy motherfucker even scared me. But I should have known better. You don't scare."

"And to warn me off he, killed Herkie."

"I didn't order it, he did it on his own. When I found out this Herkie was your friend, I went looking for the Indian myself. Never found him."

Steeg felt the flame flickering in his brain. Pretty soon, the snakes would come out to play.

Suddenly, they heard someone call.

"Dad, I've got to get back to school."

Anthony, Dave's son, was walking toward them.

Dave got to his feet. "Be there in a minute, go on back."

"But, Dad!"

Dave's face went dark. "Go on back!" He turned to Steeg. "Are we done here?"

There was one more thing. It sickened him to do it, but he couldn't carry the knowledge alone.

"Diana was Dominic and Linda's daughter," Steeg said. "She was our sister."

Dave's voice was small. "What did you say?"

"It was in the letters. When I gave Dominic Diana's picture, it all clicked. He knew what business you were in, and he figured out that she was working for you. It was a short leap after that. His son had killed the woman he'd loved and the daughter he'd never known. It was too much. For the second time, he couldn't turn you in. And he couldn't live with the knowledge of what you had done."

Dave's face turned the color of ash.

Steeg was finished; there was nothing more to say.

After several minutes, Dave broke the silence. "Where do we go from here, Jake?"

Steeg looked up. The contrails were white smudges against the blue of the sky. The road to Heaven was closed, and with it all hope for redemption. All that was left was an uncertain path into an unknown future.

A cloud passed in front of the sun, leaving them sitting in a pool of shadow.

"It's the one thing I haven't figured out yet."